A KIND MAN

Susan Hill's novels and short stories have won the Whitbread, Somerset Maugham and John Llewellyn Rhys awards and been shortlisted for the Booker Prize. She is the author of over forty books, including the Simon Serrailler crime novels. The play adapted from her famous ghost story, *The Woman in Black*, has been running on the West End stage since 1989 and the film adaptation, starring Daniel Radcliffe, is released in 2012.

Susan Hill was born in Scarborough and educated at King's College London. She is married to the Shakespeare scholar, Stanley Wells, and they have two daughters. She lives in Gloucestershire, where she runs her own small publishing company, Long Barn Books.

Susan Hill's website is www.susan-hill.com

SUSAN HILL

A Kind Man

VINTAGE BOOKS
London

Published by Vintage 2012

2 4 6 8 10 9 7 5 3 1

First published in Great Britain in 2011 by
Chatto & Windus

Vintage
Random House, 20 Vauxhall Bridge Road,
London SW1V 2SA

www.vintage-books.co.uk

Addresses for companies within The Random House Group Limited
can be found at: www.randomhouse.co.uk/offices.htm

The Random House Group Limited Reg. No. 954009

A CIP catalogue record for this book
is available from the British Library

ISBN 9780099555445

The Random House Group Limited supports The Forest Stewardship
Council (FSC®), the leading international forest certification
organisation. Our books carrying the FSC label are printed on FSC®
certified paper. FSC is the only forest certification scheme endorsed by
the leading environmental organisations, including Greenpeace. Our
paper procurement policy can be found at
www.randomhouse.co.uk/environment

Typeset by Palimpsest Book Production Ltd, Falkirk, Stirlingshire
Printed and bound by CPI Group (UK) Ltd, Croydon, CR0 4YY

A KIND MAN

I

WHEN HE had left she lay awake, the curtains still drawn together, and prayed that it would not be fine, as it always was on this day. But she could tell even through the lined blue cotton that the sun was shining. She closed her eyes for a second, against it.

There were fields then, it was all fields, and the track led directly across them from their garden gate to where it sloped up to the peak, a dry track, sometimes brown sometimes sandy sometimes grey, according to the season and the weather, but never green and grassed over.

She looked at the peak, touched by the sun.

Then she washed and brushed her hair, coiled it up and pinned it, and at last went downstairs.

The spray of plum blossom was on the kitchen

table, thickly clotted white and set carefully in the best china jug, as usual. She touched the petals, but they were too delicate for the roughened pad of her forefinger to feel them.

The sunlight touched them as it touched the peak. Nothing would be said.

The tin bowl of scraps and meal was on the ledge, waiting from the previous night when she had filled it, last thing before going up to bed, the chickens being her job and nothing to do with Tommy at all except for the wringing of necks. She used to do that. She had done a lot of things.

Once she had unlatched the door and stepped outside and felt the sun on her face and that the sun had a little warmth in it, she did not mind it after all and forgot she had prayed for rain and greyness. And that was as always too.

The past winter had been hard. Christmas was wild gales and then the snow had come straight after and piled up against the door and the henhouse, the fence and the gate. Tommy had had to dig himself a path out in the morning so that he could get to work, and the fields had been a foot deep in it, he had to set off an hour early just to be sure of making the time. From late grey dawns to early sunset the wind had blown at the cottage from the north-east, finding out every hair's-breadth crack and crevice in windows and door and roof slates, even, it sometimes felt, in the walls themselves. The range had been full all day and all night, gobbling up the fuel and yet never seeming to get warm. He had lit a fire in the front room too, but even when that had blazed up, drawn by the brisk wind down the chimney, their breath had been white as ghost-breath on the air, a yard distance from the hearth. The inside of every window was glazed with ice, the icicles hung down, gleaming crystal spikes, and the chickens' water dish had to be hammered until the shards flew. Eve had sat huddled over the range, fringing scarves with stiff, sore fingers.

The chickens started up as she opened the door, clucking round in circles and, as she approached down the path to their pen, flapping their wings. It was difficult to empty the tin, they tried to attack it and her so vigorously, but once the first scraps were on the ground and they were pecking at them, she could step back and enjoy it. Tommy had long given up puzzling out why she liked them, gave them names, admired the gleam on their feathers and their strutting and jerky movements. 'Only you don't mind them in the oven or on the plate,' he often said. But that was different, it was the way of things. It was just the killing she could no longer do. That and other things.

3

She stood for some time, alternately watching the fowl and looking round her, looking at the beginnings of the year's kitchen garden taking shape, the first rows freshly dug, the bean canes he had started tying, and then beyond, at the field and the track and the sunlight on the peak.

It was all fields then.

2

HER NAME had been Eve Gooch and she had lived in Water Street which ran alongside the canal. The bedroom she shared with her sister Miriam had looked onto it. Every morning when the curtains were drawn back there was the wide, black-shining water moving soundlessly past. Occasionally you saw a duck or even a swan, often a barge pulling coal or scrap metal, but otherwise there was only the dark, slick water.

She left at seven to meet three others on the corner from where they walked, arm in arm and head-scarved, across town to the pottery. Miriam went the other way to the printworks. Their mother stayed at home. Their father was dead before Miriam was four years old. She barely remembered him. Eve had a recollection of a man with stubble beard and smelling of clean carbolic soap, a man with a loud voice but a calm way. And then he was gone.

Miriam had met hers first. John Bullard, very tall, very thin, with a long nose and an odd turn in his eye, John Bullard who spoke very little, smiled instead, or nodded or shook his head.

'How did you ever get him to look round at you, least of all ask you out?' Eve had said when her sister had first come home to wash all over and change into her lemon silk blouse. 'How did he make himself understood?'

Miriam had reddened and turned her back in their small room, but later, going down the stairs in her best shoes, she had said, 'He can be quite talkative when he likes.'

Eve and their mother had exchanged glances. 'He can be quite talkative.' Disbelief, the inability to apply the description to John Bullard, had united them as few things did.

Afterwards, Eve thought that she had willed Tommy Carr into her life because of her dread of being left alone with their mother when Miriam married. They were only fifteen months apart in age – Eve the elder – and she never once begrudged Miriam her husband-to-be, their house, their future,

6

only, without ever forming it into so many words, determined that she, would follow on.

There had been whistles and looks and quiet hand-holding at dances in the Victoria Hall and once, an arm round her shoulders and a quick kiss on a ride at All Hallows Fair, but no one who had taken to her, no one she had given a second glance.

John Bullard had come to tea twice a week and he and Miriam had taken over the front room, but with the door always kept ajar as their mother insisted, though Eve had no interest in prying and spying and kept to the bedroom or went out. It was late summer and still hot in the days, with soft balmy evenings, so that she could walk to the far end of the street and then cut down the snicket to the canal towpath, where there were always people strolling, couples, men on their way to and from the pubs and the Legion, children playing out late, boys fishing. She liked the sense of comrade-ship on these evenings, everyone belonging to the same place, working and living and playing and walking, so that they exchanged a word and a greeting whether they knew one another by name or sight or not. Because they belonged. Eve never felt this at other times. She had no real sense of where she lived, no affiliation to it. It was. She lived and worked here, always had, so always would and that was all there was to it.

But on these late-summer evenings it was different.

There was something in the air of the place that gave her small spurts of a hopefulness and promise, an excitement even, that were otherwise unfamiliar.

Miriam and John Bullard were married when the evenings had drawn in and there were the first frosts, but the day had been clear and bright with sunshine that made everything hard-edged. It had been a rush of working until well into every night to get the wedding dress and Eve's dress finished, the sewing machine trundling for hours and the kitchen table covered with a sheet and then with the white lace and the blue satin, the tin of pins and the box of buttons and the sprays of artificial mimosa and pearls sewn onto a headband that held the veil.

Eve wore the blue satin with a small hat pinned perilously to the side of her head.

John Bullard's suit was shiny and his hair shone too, flattened well down, which emphasised his nose and the boniness of his face. His hands were huge, Eve noticed, as he held her sister's to fit the ring.

They left at three, driven to the station by John Bullard's uncle, and by five people had left and the church hall was a mess of cake crumbs and empty cups. A streamer which had hung across the room had come unpinned and was dangling down and her footsteps made a hollow tapping sound on the boards as she helped to clear up.

Her mother had drunk three glasses of sherry and her eyes were too bright. Eve felt odd and dispirited.

So that was a wedding, she thought.

A week later, she met Tommy Carr, and afterwards, she had felt as if everything was falling out as easily as the cards can fall out suddenly, in a game of patience, one after another after another into place. It had been quite straightforward. She had to take a skirt her mother had altered to a woman who lived on the east side of the town and she went by the canal path and was walking towards the footbridge when a stray dog came racing towards her and stopped, to whirl barking and barking round her feet. The skirt was wrapped in brown paper and tied with string and in her efforts to be free of the barking dog she had slipped. She had righted herself at once but the parcel had flown from her hand into the canal and the dog had leaped into the water after it, still barking, swimming as it had jumped, round and round in an ecstasy of excitement.

The dog's owner had reached her at the same moment as a man had run down the steps of the footbridge and together, while Eve watched, they had hooked the parcel with an overhanging tree branch they had snapped off. After the parcel, swung dripping with water onto the path, had come the dog, hauled by its collar. Eve had seen its legs paddling furiously and then its open mouth as it had scrambled out of the canal. The dog had seemed to be laughing, its bark interrupted by an abrupt cough as it spat out a mouthful of water.

And then it was over and calm and the dog was gone and Eve was left looking in dismay at the soaking wet brown-paper parcel on the path.

A couple of years before, Nelly Holmes, her mother's oldest friend, had thought of remarrying. It had been a long time since she had lost her husband and hard bringing up three boys alone. He had asked. She had hesitated. Come to their house.

They had all been in, sitting round the table after tea, with scarves laid out for fringing and a sheet to hem. But Miriam had been delaying, wanting her game of patience to come out and it would not.

'No, no, don't send them off,' Nelly Holmes had said, sitting down and catching her breath, stout woman that she was. 'It isn't private.' Though it was, they could tell straight away, and their mother had kept glancing at them uneasily for fear of them catching a phrase they shouldn't hear.

Miriam had gone on trying to get the patience out,

not interested. Eve had fiddled with the scarf, wishing she could leave, not quite knowing how, not wanting to hear the talk, embarrassed, though that precise word was not known to her then.

But after a moment, she had begun to listen and to think about Nelly Holmes, with her three growing boys in the tiny terrace house, toilet at the far end of the narrow garden, precious little money.

'It might make such a difference,' she was saying, 'such a difference. They need a man about the place and it would be a wage. Besides, I'd like some company.'

And there was more, this good reason and that. Vera Gooch had listened in silence, looking at her friend's face now and then but letting her come to the end like a thread running out and the shuttle gradually slowing to a halt.

The room had subsided into quiet. Miriam's cards made a soft pat as she set them down one by one.

At last, Vera had got up. The old cat was at the window waiting to be let in.

Vera had looked round at Nelly Holmes. 'Only the one thing I'd ask,' she had said. 'Which you maybe haven't thought of or can even answer and you should.'

Not only Nelly, but Eve and Miriam too waited now, looking at her, Miriam's hand frozen on the cards.

'Is he a kind man?'

Somehow, it took them all by surprise. It was not what they had been expecting, which had perhaps been a thought of money or work or an existing family, where they might live, Nelly Holmes's old father. Any of that.

Is he a kind man?

Yet Eve had seen at once that it was the only question that mattered and contained everything else within itself and Nelly's reply.

Is he a kind man?

The rest would follow. Or it would not.

3

Tommy Carr was a kind man, she had been able to tell that after half an hour of knowing him – kind to help her unpack the parcel and see that the skirt inside was not even damp, kind to suggest that she fold it carefully and take it as it was, not so much as mentioning the paper and string. Kind to come with her in case the woman whose skirt it was might chastise or blame her, and then he could help Eve explain. Kind to walk home with her just to the end of the street but no further, so as to spare her any looks and questions.

Kind.

And so it had been, she thought, looking at the sprays of plum blossom he had left ready for her in the jug, as always, and knowing what he felt without a word needing to be said. There had never been a day when he had not shown her some small kindness or spoken a kind word. It was what he was and not only to her, it was his nature, everyone said so. People spoke of him as kind Tommy Carr. He had been a kind boy, they said, his mother and aunt and neighbours and friends and workpeople who had known him all his life, kind to smaller children, to creatures, to someone hurt or shy or who caught the wrong end of the teacher's tongue or the flat blade of the ruler.

There was nothing else memorable about him. He was neither good- nor bad-looking. He had short straight brown hair and a pleasant face you forgot the moment you turned your back. If you wanted to point out anything it would be the pale scar across his upper lip where he had been bitten by a ferret. He was neither tall nor short, he was thin but not awkwardly so. There was nothing in the way he moved to distinguish him. But his voice was quiet and he never wasted words. Words, he said, could be dangerous and too little respected.

Her mother had let out a soft little whimper when she had taken Tommy Carr home the first time. Eve knew what the whimper signified. 'Not you. Not you as well. First Miriam, now . . .'

But the whole truth was not just that she did not want to be left alone, it was as much that she had never liked John Bullard and made it clear as clear.

He was, variously 'lazy' and 'overcareful' and he paid her too little attention. The best she had ever been heard to say was that he was 'nothing special'. But from the first moment he had stepped through the front door, Tommy Carr had become everything John Bullard was not. He was raised to ridiculous heights of virtue and importance from which he could surely only topple.

It had been alarming because Eve herself was not as sure about Tommy as her mother appeared to be, for all that she had recognised him at once as 'a kind man'. But kindness was only one of many desirable qualities, at the age of twenty, she thought necessary in a young man, let alone in a husband, and she had searched for those each time they met.

She could not have said what it was that she wanted but sometimes pinned it down to the word 'spark'. He had no spark. He was steady, quiet, calm, reliable, loyal, thoughtful, gentle. A kind man then. But for a long time she resisted those things in favour of something he lacked and which she felt there must surely be.

'Spark,' she had said once to Miriam. Her sister, pregnant by then and tired and shocked by how much work there was to be done in a day looking after a house and a man, had snorted in derision.

'You marry him when he asks,' their mother said

over and again, 'you see sense. Men like Tommy Carr don't grow on trees.'

'He maybe won't ask and even if he did . . .'

But he asked soon enough, as Eve had known that he would, known, she realised, from the moment he had helped her unwrap the waterlogged parcel on the canal bank. To see so clearly and without possibility of choice into her own future was terrifying.

It had been the last time, it occurred to her now, that she was seriously afraid of anything, anything at all, for when she married Tommy Carr she moved into a protected circle. She had even thought that nothing could ever hurt her again, but that had not been true, nor should it have been. Pain and hurt were not his to prevent, or so it had seemed, but what he gave her was peace of mind and a reassurance about life, a steadiness. She could even face small things that had once terrified her – large spiders and lightning storms, stray dogs and things people did that she had been brought up to believe were unlucky. Now, if shoes were put on the table or lilac brought into the house, she simply removed the shoes because they belonged on the floor and found a jug for the blossom.

Living with Tommy affected everything about her, changed and strengthened and calmed her, and led her quietly out of childhood and girlhood into adult life. Her mother had been right. The question of whether Eve loved him did not arise for a long time, simply because there were so many other benefits to her marriage. Miriam had talked about love endlessly, before John Bullard and after they met. Eve did not. Only one day, after they had been married for a year, she had unpegged his shirt from the line and suddenly put it to her face to smell the cleanness and been suffused with the sense that it was his shirt and therefore important because of love. She loved. It was as obvious as the blueness of the sky and her state of plain contentment had become one of happiness in a single moment.

4

S HE OPENED the door and looked across to the peak.
The early sun had risen higher and was bathing
the garden. The hens clucked.

Why did she feel it would be any better if the sky
turned curded grey and the rain came on? It had
sometimes been like that, or else a bitter wind
had cut round her head as she had walked, but it had
made no difference, any more than the spring sun
and warmth.

How could it? It scarcely mattered.

That day had been fine, with this lapis sky above
the peak and the sun warm on her face.

That day.

She filled the kettle and left it on the back of the
range for her return and then took the sprays of plum
blossom out of the jug, shook the water off the stems

and wrapped them tightly in a couple of sheets of newspaper.

There was no one about. By this time in the morning those who went to work had gone and children to school, those who stayed at home were washing and cooking and scrubbing the floors, changing the beds, shaking out dusters, setting the bones and the veg in a pan for stock. Later, they would be out, pegging washing, taking a moment to sit at the open back door in the sun. You always took the moment.

There were six in a row, called cottages but really just small brick houses like the brick houses in the town, the brick houses she and Tommy had been born and brought up in. But someone had thought to set a row out here on the edge of the fields and looking towards the peak. From the back, you could see the smoke from the factory chimneys, and if the wind was this way, hear the faint roar of the furnaces and the thump of the machines. But from the front it was the field and the track across it to the peak. Beyond the peak was another world to which they went sometimes on Sundays, walking over the soft mounded hills. None of them was like the peak, which stood alone as an outcrop, jagged and steep. The peak, marked the change between the two worlds.

*　*　*

19

She did not lock the door. No one ever did. A locked door was an insult to a visitor who, if there was no reply, might try the handle and put a head round, call out, but leave again at once if there was no answer. If a door was locked it was like a slap in the face. Only if you went away you might lock and leave a key with a neighbour. But who went away?

She shut the gate and set off, across the wide empty field, the plum blossom in her hand pointing downwards to the ground. The sky seemed huge and to grow wider as she reached the middle. From here, there was only a thin haze in the distance and a faint rising plume of smoke to mark the town. It was a walk of two miles and she took it three times every year, at Christmas, in August and on this day, which was the one that counted. Once, she had had pneumonia at Christmas, one August Tommy's mother had died and she had been forced to miss, but somehow it had not mattered greatly. It was understood. She had never missed this April day and never would as long as her legs could bear her.

The track reached the foot of the peak and then forked into two, narrower paths, one going straight ahead up the steep slope and the other around the base of it to the far side. Eve paused. A lark, so high that she could not see it, was streaming out a song that came spiralling down to her through empty space.

Far above the peak, two buzzards soared silently, flat wings outstretched like windmill sails. Tommy had never been with her and never spoken to her about it either, but she knew well that it was not for any want of feeling but for an excess of it, overflowing but somehow damned up inside him. She did not lay any blame. If he had ever forgotten and not gone out to cut the branch of blossom for her to bring, perhaps that would be the time for blame. But he would never forget, she could be sure of that.

She walked slowly because she needed to feel herself getting nearer a little at a time, making the journey as people made a pilgrimage and because, in spite of her usual prayer for grey skies, once she was out here she savoured the spring air and the sun and the smell of the new earth and the growing things, loved to hear the larks. As she rounded the peak, she looked up and ahead to the far slope where the sheep were with their lambs, dozens of them scattered about the hillside like scraps of paper thrown up in the air and allowed to settle anywhere. If there was a wind it usually blew their bleating towards her but today it was quite still. She only heard the soft sound of her footsteps on the track.

The slope was gentle and after a half-mile, at the point where an old plough had been abandoned and lay knotted over with bindweed and grass, she could see the church tower. It had four flying angels on each corner and they caught the sun and shone gold. But today, just as she looked up to them, skeins of cloud were drawn across and the angels were dulled.

Centuries before there had been a large village up here, but it had been deserted after a plague and re-established further down on the far side, and the church had been left stranded by itself among ruins which had gradually fallen away and disappeared. But the church was never abandoned and services were even held in it half a dozen times each summer. People valued it. Guidebooks referred to what had become known as 'St Paul-Alone' or 'St Paul-in-the Meadow'. Once or twice a visitor had been there when Eve had arrived and perhaps smiled or exchanged a word. The first time she had thought that she might mind, but she had not, there was a friendliness about having others here and she welcomed it, always looked out to see if people might be there.

She walked more slowly still up the last few yards. There was no stone wall, though perhaps it had once been there, no gate or entrance, no shady trees. The church stood alone with its tower rising up strongly and the angels flying freely in the wind, and for a path there was simply a worn track up to the door. And on two sides the churchyard, which was part of the hillside, part of the whole wide landscape, not penned in or confined, and the ancient gravestones set out anyhow, like the sheep on the opposite hill. Ancient but for a handful. The village was all but gone save for three or four cottages. Now and then a person died but few were buried here.

The first time she had ever come, quite by chance and years ago, Eve had felt a strange surge of rightness and belonging, something she had never known before. They went to church as a family for Christmas and Easter, she and her sister had been baptised and confirmed in the parish church in the centre of the town, a great, granite place with a chill in its bones. She had always felt a formal reverence and respect but never any closeness.

So that when the time had come, she had unhesitatingly picked St Paul-Alone for the burial. There had never been a doubt, and Tommy had gone along with her wishes, knowing how she felt. He had a deep sense of what was good and even holy but no connection with any church or chapel.

No one else was here. The sheeps' cries and the bleating of the lambs came to her now on the wind. Another lark sang high out of sight.

No one had understood why she had chosen this place and she had not felt able to explain, just insisted over and over again that it must be, and Tommy had agreed and stood by her even if he too had not fully understood. It was others who murmured together and felt resentful. She had ignored them and never for one moment regretted what she had done. Her feelings had been absolute and could not have been gainsaid.

The path was grassy and dry. They had not had heavy rain for weeks. Her footsteps made a soft brushing sound as she stepped over the old, leaning grave-stones, patched with yellow and grey sponge moss and lichen. Some had lettering too worn to be read, others had whole words obscured. Some she now knew by heart.

Joseph Garnett. Born 1802. Died 1870.
And his wife Adeline.
'And he shall stand at the latter day.'

In loving memory of Samuel Pettifer.
And of Mary Pettifer of this parish.
And their children Maud, Archibald, Victoria.

She stopped again to wonder as always who Mary Pettifer was, wife or mother or daughter, and why her dates of birth and death had not been carved.

Surgeon Captain Makin Lownes,
a gallant officer and comrade.
Born 1789. Died at sea, 1824.

One by one she counted them, read them, set them aside, and so, slowly, made her way to the far end.

It was set a little apart from the old graves, but the stone no longer looked raw and smooth, the wind and rain that drove up the hill in winter had pitted and darkened it.

There was a shallow rectangle cut from the grass and edged with more cut stone laid flat.

Eve held her breath for a moment. Whenever she saw it again, at the moment she read the lettering, her heart seemed to stop in its beating. The first few times she had longed for it never to start up again.

Jeannie Eliza Carr
Aged 3 years
Beloved daughter

She knelt down and brushed a few leaves away, then laid the branches of white blossom carefully down on the grass.

5

A T FIRST they had lived with Tommy's mother in the terraces behind the works and Eve had dreaded it, being shy and not knowing how Rose Carr liked things and how she would fit into the household. But it was easy enough, though crowded. Tommy had a brother with whom he had used to share a room and Alan had had to move into the box room. He had not seemed to resent it, or even to notice, but Eve had felt uncomfortable and after a few months only they had moved out when one of the houses on the opposite side of the terrace came free. It was pleasant enough and she tried to make the best of it but it was dark morning, noon and night, because the works buildings loomed over it and, having a north aspect, no room was ever lightened by the sun.

She was happy with Tommy Carr. He was indeed

'a kind man', thoughtful, quiet, gentle, undemanding, eating anything that was put in front of him, tidy and clean, unwilling to put her to any trouble, and, unlike every other man she knew of or had known, glad to help her in the house. He would not only fetch in the coals and deal with the fires and the range but set the table and clear it, bring in the washing from the line and clean both his own shoes and hers. They liked one another. They were suited.

But from the beginning both had been clear that they wanted a child, 'to make a family' as he said, 'out of the two of us'.

After seven months in the dark house no child had been conceived, and Eve had struggled with herself through the long autumn and winter of early dark and grey skies, low-spirited and lacking in interest for anything in the small rooms whose walls pressed in on her 'like coffin sides', she said one evening.

Tommy laid down his knife and fork and looked across the tea table at her, his face troubled and full of concern.

'That's a strong thing to say.'

'Yes.'

'You feel it that badly then?'

She did. She had, she now knew, been 'feeling it that badly' for some time.

He said nothing more until he brought the stack of

dishes in and set them on the wooden draining board beside her. Then he put his hand on her shoulder.

'You should have said.'

'No, no, it's nothing.'

'That isn't how it sounded.'

'I don't want to worry you, Tom. I'm just having a down day.'

He went out again and she finished the dishes, set them to drain, looked out of the window onto the gathering sky and saw rain spots dashing against the window.

He had stoked up the range to a blaze and set their chairs closer to it, put a cushion for Eve's back, which she had hurt in turning round too sharply the previous week. She brought in fresh cups of tea.

The evening paper was beside him as usual, but after only a glance he set it quietly down.

'It's the house,' he said, 'the dark that gets you down.'

'Oh, it'll be better when the days lengthen, take no notice of me.'

'Of course I take notice of you. Besides, winter or summer, the works is still there and you can't turn a house around.'

She smiled. There were his work socks to darn in the basket at her feet but she went on drinking her tea and looking into the fire.

'I know what I should do.'

'What's that?'

'Move us. Move you to where it's light and open and you can breathe a bit. That'd be the best thing, and for a bairn when one wants to come to us as well. Maybe that's why. It's thinking it won't put in an appearance to be brought up in a coal-hole.'

He had made little of the absence of a child, re-assuring her that one would come when it was ready, though she could not be so easy in her mind now that Miriam had two boys and a third expected and was wondering how to stop.

She could hardly talk to her sister, hardly visit them because her envy spurted up like bile in her mouth.

She went sometimes to the great dark granite church to ask for the gift of a child and liked it better when she sat there alone rather than at the services which they occasionally went to. Miriam's babies were christened there and each one had cried. 'It's cold,' Eve had said, 'that's why they cry. It's never been warm inside that place in all its history.'

Perhaps, she sometimes thought, God had deserted it Himself for that very reason.

'I'll find us somewhere,' Tommy had said that evening, and being a man of his word, a week later, he had done so, though not telling her at first, just suggesting they walk out that Saturday afternoon. It had been a fine day, blowy and chill, but as they had left the town streets and started off towards the first fields that hemmed it round she had felt her spirits lighten.

He had looked at her. 'Your cheeks have got pink now,' he had said, 'in the fresher air.'

Though you could still smell the factory chimneys and taste the smoke faintly in your mouth.

'Look.'

He had pointed to the terrace of six brick houses facing the field and the peak further away.

'Look where?'

'There.'

'Houses.'

He laughed.

But he had led her to them and walked along to the last one, on the end and so with open fields on three sides. For a moment they had stood looking at it, a small, neat, plain house with a long ruler of garden running from the door, which was painted a dark red.

'I thought it good,' Tommy said.

'Good.'

'For us.'

'It would be.'

'So we'll take it then? It's for rent.'

They had moved in the following week, and from the first day, Eve had felt happy. The house was only a little bigger than their old one in the town but it felt vast because of the light – light flooded in front and back and because there was nothing overshadowing them any more, nothing taller than their house apart from the peak and that you could see but at a distance.

She had stood looking and looking, at the fields and the track that led across them and the slope and the sky, and had felt a different person.

'But you'd have a way to go to work,' she had said that first afternoon.

'I don't mind a walk. I can do up the old bike as well if I find my own legs too slow.'

He did not mind. He got up forty minutes earlier and walked. Eve watched him set off across the track that led back to the town, his stride calm and steady, before beginning her work in the house, and then the minute she could, going outside to the garden. It had been dug over and made before but then left to weed and neglect, but day by day she shaped it and cleared it and then began to plan what to grow. The man next door had brought round things to start her off, cuttings and plants, bits of this and that. And advice. Bert Ankerby. His wife Mary grew fat red geraniums and tomatoes on all the window ledges and gave cuttings of those too. When Eve had spoken of chickens, Bert had told her where to go for a couple and he and Tommy had put together the henhouse and run.

Every day she woke up feeling happy in a way she had never known before. She loved her husband, her home, her life.

A couple of months after they had moved into what was known only as 6 The Cottages, Miriam had a third son, but in giving birth to him was gravely ill and both she and the baby had to be taken to hospital where they stayed for several weeks, Miriam lying between life and death. But the baby thrived and because of Miriam's illness and an epidemic of scarlet fever in the hospital it was thought better for him to go home. John Bullard sent for Eve.

For five weeks she left Tommy to look after himself and 6 The Cottages and became mother to two boys and the baby, Arthur George, though the worst trouble was John Bullard, who did nothing, either for himself or his children, but came in at five and sat down, expecting the tea to be in front of him, his glass of beer at his side, went out to the working men's club or the public house and came in at ten. Cocoa, bread and meat or cheese had to be waiting for him. He did not drink much ale, only went for the company of other men and because he hated sitting in the house that smelled of boiling and small boys. He was not mean. He handed Eve his wage packet as he always handed it to his wife, and told her what he expected back for himself. He was friendly towards her and grateful to her, but he lifted no finger to help her and took little notice of the boys. The baby he left entirely to her. Arthur George might not have existed for all the times he so much as glanced at him. The boy grew and roared for food and slept deeply and his brothers absorbed him into their midst without comment.

Eve was exhausted and felt her spirits dampened not only by the work and the tiredness but by the return to the closed-in town and the smell of the chimney stacks. Three or four times a week, Tommy came down to help her and took the boys out with him as well, walked them up to 6 The Cottages and let them loose, to race about the field, and taught them how to feed the chickens and collect the eggs, handle the rabbit and dig up the vegetables. He wore them out on those days and with only herself and the baby in the strangely quiet house, Eve felt calmer and sat with Arthur George in the crook of her arm or across her lap, stroking his thistledown hair and looking at the pink fingernails. His hands were large already, like those of his father, wide and stubby, not the hands of a baby at all. But the nails were delicate and almost translucent. She could see the flow of blood beneath the surface.

It was a hard time but she had no choice in the matter of filling her sister's place and did not resent it, and when Miriam finally came home, Eve stayed on another two weeks, because it was plain that Miriam had little strength or energy. She had been plump and now she was thin, ruddy and her skin was sallow.

'You've done so well for him, Eve,' she said over and again, looking at the baby in his crib but making no move to lift him up. 'You've done so well for them all.'

'I hope I have.'

'What would they have done? John would have been lost.'

Eve said nothing but thanked God silently for her own husband and his help and strength.

She prayed too that Miriam did not have another child, not because she herself would resent it but because Miriam would surely never have the strength now to carry another and look after the rest. Eve wished she could say something, warn or at least show her concern. But they did not talk about such things together.

6

IT WAS a whole year more before she herself became pregnant, but now that she was happy in 6 The Cottages she did not fret about it or become low-spirited when month after month went by. It would come about in its own good time, she had no doubt now, though if anyone had asked her why and she had had to say that it was because of the house and the light she would have felt foolish.

In the meantime, their lives went steadily on. The garden took shape. Everything grew well the first season and better the next, the chickens gave them too many eggs so she took a basket of them into the town every week, and after leaving some for Miriam and her mother, she sold the rest to the butcher in Salt Lane and got a good price. The money went partly into savings, which they had never before had, and partly for things she bought to make the house nice, fabric for curtains and cushions, some better pans, and occasionally some small piece of old china, a jug or a cup and saucer that she picked up on a market stall or in the bric-a-brac shop. She liked delicate pieces with roses on or dark blue bands with gilding and set them out on the dresser and the rougher pieces on the kitchen window ledge filled with flowers and bits of greenery. They caught the sun. Once a week she took them carefully down piece by piece and washed and dried them until they shone.

John Bullard acquired a car, which no one else in the family or even in the street had ever had, and twice drove Miriam and the children to 6 The Cottages, for the boys to let off steam in the field and Miriam to sit in the sun on the back step, watching Eve working at the garden until she too sat down and they felt like kids again, a bottle of lemonade between them and their sleeves rolled up to try and brown their arms.

Once, looking sideways at her as she was speaking, Eve saw how much older her sister seemed. She was not so thin or so pale as before but her face had somehow changed, fallen in a little, and she had grey hairs and looked too much like their mother.

'If I had another one I'd kill myself,' she said.

'That's a terrible thing to say. How can you bring yourself to speak like that?'

'You could have it if you wanted then.'

Eve was silent.

'You looked after them fine. They were happy.'

'All the same.'

'All the same nothing. I mean it. The doctors said I'd probably die anyway.'

Eve did not know whether to believe her or not. Miriam had been given to lying when they were girls.

From the field they heard the boys whooping and shouting.

'They love it up here,' Miriam said.

'I love it.'

'Aren't you lucky?'

Eve had never before heard her sound bitter in that way.

The day drifted down into a soft warm evening. The boys came back covered in what Eve thought of as clean dirt, dust from the track and the sandy burrows under the far hedge, and helped her feed and shut up the chickens and by the time John Bullard came for them it was dark and they were asleep and had to be lifted in to the back seat of the old car. Miriam sat in front, and did not so much as glance back.

* * *

Eve's own pregnancy was without incident and she felt well after the first weeks, walked every day across the track towards the peak because the autumn was early and chill but bright and walking was easy. It was how she found the church, walking when she was not yet too heavy to do the two miles and back without discomfort. It was late November. She had never been to the other side of the peak but once she found the church, stranded alone like a ship at sea, she went several more times, wandering round the graveyard reading the stones that could be read, before going inside where it was dim and cold, and smelled of the earth. Once, she had brought Tommy and there had been a service, the church lit by candles and only one other person there besides the parson. It was the last time, he told them, when the winter came it was impossibly cold and if it snowed, no one could reach it. Eve thought of it often in January, trapped in whiteness and cold, waiting for the spring to bring it to life again.

Tommy went steadily through the days, and though he was caring of her, did not fuss or cause her any anxiety. He looked forward as she did but he was a man to focus on the present and take the future as it came to him. But she could tell by the way he glanced at her, took over the lifting and hen feeding, made her tea before he left each morning, that he felt some small anxiety. What had happened to Miriam had shocked them both. Nothing could ever quite be taken for granted again.

7

H ER LABOUR, beginning in the early hours of a Sunday morning, was short and fierce. There was no time for Tommy to run for the midwife, but hearing the sounds, Mary Ankerby came, in time to see the child, a small, dark-haired girl, lying next to Eve on the bed, mad as a wasp and still attached to the cord, which Mary cut deftly, having had seven of her own and all born at 5 The Cottages.

'And what better place to start in life?' she said, handing the girl to Eve, who lay dazed, the birth not having been expected for another week.

'Jeannie,' Tommy had said from the beginning. 'Jeannie Eliza,' though where the names had come from Eve did not know for there was no one called either in their families.

Jeannie Eliza Carr lay tight-swaddled in the white

flannel sheet like a small chrysalis, dark blue eyes looking out. Tommy drew the curtain against the first sun streaming in through the window onto them but Eve made him pull it back again, wanting their daughter to be touched by it and to have a sight of the wide sky.

From the first, she was a quiet, watching child, only crying for her needs, and when they were satisfied, lying peacefully, not always sleeping, and as she grew, always looking for her father at the sound of his voice, following his movements. For years he had played the fiddle, though he did not know music. An Irishman who had worked for a while in the town had taught him, and when he had moved on, left Tommy his own violin, saying that when he got back home he could always pick up another. Tommy had played the dances and jigs and occasional slow sad tearful ballads he had heard and, getting gradually more tuneful and confident, taken to entertaining people outside in the street or the public house. He became in demand for wakes and weddings, though everyone knew what he would play, his repertoire being limited. But they waited for the next tune to come round in its turn and sang or danced to it cheerfully, so that if he had suddenly presented them with something new they would have felt uneasy.

When he met Eve he had played less and at 6 The Cottages had only taken out his fiddle once or twice, there was so much to do at first and then he got out of the way of it. But on the day of his daughter's birth he fetched it from the upstairs cupboard and tuned it carefully, before drawing his bow tentatively and softly across the strings. At once, Eve had seen that Jeannie listened intently, and after that, every time he played, sitting outside so as not to startle her, she had seemed barely to breathe. If she was restless or teething or sleepless his playing would always settle her.

'I like to hear the music,' Mary said, looking over. If Eve had to walk into the town, Mary would have the baby, who seemed to fit into the world of 5 as easily as of 6 The Cottages.

The day after Jeannie was born, John Bullard had brought Miriam in the car, the boys pouring out of the back of it and straight into the field, like caged birds set free. It was a fine day and Eve sat propped on pillows in the bed, the window open a little, Jeannie asleep in the crib beside her. As her sister came into the room Eve saw the look on her face, of bitterness and weariness, and she put out her hand to her, feeling ashamed for a moment of her own contentment, and of having the daughter she knew Miriam longed for, though she had never spoken a word of it. Miriam glanced into the crib and glanced away.

Every time she came she seemed older, as if she

were a soft stone that was being worn down, its surface thinning and giving way. Her face was the colour of dirty paper, her hands red and roughened, the nails cracked. But she had put a slide in her hair and a brooch on her frock.

'Jeannie Eliza,' she said, standing at the window. 'Where's that from?'

'Tommy. He named her. It just came to him – because he liked it.'

'You were all over quick.'

'I was. I suppose it's one way or the other and you have no say in the matter.'

Miriam said nothing.

'They'll come to no harm,' Eve said, thinking she was anxious for the boys romping out. Tommy and John Bullard were both there, and the boys could be heard shouting with laughter.

Miriam turned to face her, 'What if they did.'

'Miriam!'

'And you so smug with yourself.'

Eve bit her lip. Jeannie stirred slightly like a leaf in the breeze, and then was still. Her eyelids were streaked pale violet-blue.

'You wait till you've four like me.'

'You've only three.'

But she saw it on Miriam's face and did not know what to say.

'You try and put a stop to it,' Miriam said.

'But you were so ill with Arthur George.'

Her sister shrugged.

Tommy made tea and bread and butter and jam and there were rock buns brought round warm by Mary. The boys tumbled in and took what they wanted in their hands and went out again. Miriam brought Eve tea and a plate of food. When she came in, Eve had the baby to her breast.

'It wears you down,' she said.

Eve could not say that she would have sat like this for the rest of her life, with the baby's soft mouth gripping round her like a sea anemone and the small hands there too, the fingers splayed out on her flesh.

'I'd give them away.'

Eve stared at her. She had never liked it when people said such teasing things too easily. 'Words,' Tommy would say. But from Miriam's face she saw that it was not a tease, not something said lightly when she was down.

'That's terrible. You shouldn't say any such thing. You love them.'

Miriam sighed. 'Oh yes. But how does that change matters?'

Jeannie Eliza made a tiny sound.

'You cherish her.'

'Miriam, you shouldn't –'

'Don't you tell me what I should and should not do,' she blazed up. 'You were always good at that. Don't you dare. What do you know?'

Eve looked down at the soft spot on the top of the baby's head, the pale membrane stretched across like the skin on top of an egg.

'Oh, her. You've got her so you think you know it all.'

'No.'

'You'll learn, you and that mother's boy Tommy.'

Perhaps she should have felt anger and shouted at Miriam, sent her packing, defended Tommy for his being a kind man and quiet. But what good would that have done? She felt Miriam's own rage, and the hurt and jealousy coming from her like hot breath, and knew that enough had been said and that she herself must simply absorb it all and not strike back.

The chink of dishes came from the kitchen below. Tommy would be clearing away and washing up, John Bullard sitting back. The boys' shouts came from far across the field.

The baby had gone to sleep, her mouth letting the nipple droop.

'Would you like to hold her now?'

Miriam turned away. 'Why would I want to do that? I've had plenty of it and more to come.'

But from the doorway she said, 'She's very bonny, Eve.'

They left soon after, the boys wailing in protest. Miriam did not come back upstairs.

'I don't know,' Tommy said, taking her teacup away. He touched his daughter's soft hair wonderingly with the back of his finger as he passed.

Eve did not tell him. Miriam would do nothing, it had been a sudden despairing moment, but she surely would not do anything. Yet she had barely said one pleasant word, not admired the baby, nor given her sister a word of praise, which seemed to Eve a sad, bitter thing.

8

LATER THAT year they started laying off men, first in the coach and next in the brickworks and after that the closures spread to the mills. A dozen went, then fifty, then half. John Bullard was one of the early ones to go and by then he and Miriam had four boys and no money coming in. Vera Gooch had a little set by and helped them. Tommy, whose wages were still good, called in and left a shilling every time in the teacup on the sideboard, not wanting to be discovered or to put them to shame. The whole town seemed to be sliding into a pit of despair, though people tried to put on brave faces and talk one another round, the women at their doors, the men on the street corners or, if they had a few pence, in the public houses and their own clubs. It was no worse here than in most places.

'When is it coming to us?' Eve asked. Jeannie Eliza was pulling herself along the rug to try and reach the little stray cat which had come in one night from a hailstorm and never left. 'We can't always be in luck.'

Though the printworks had plenty on still and Tommy even did extra hours because he was one of the most skilled men, he knew how the machines ran and could save a fortune because in his hands they never broke down.

But he only told her not to fret and picked up the baby to take her out and show her the rabbit before he locked it up. He carried her as often as he could, she was up and in his arms the moment he got in unless she was asleep, and when she was fretful, which was rarely enough, he got out the fiddle and played her a soft tune, or spoke to her, old rhymes and tales he remembered from his own childhood, and she watched him out of dark blue eyes.

That was a dreadful winter, with the granite-grey church setting up trestle tables in the porch and serving soup and bread and cheese and having long queues, the Baptist chapel giving out shoes and warm scarves to families with children. No one could think ahead to Christmas.

John Bullard was goaded by Miriam into joining the line of men looking for work and after a few weeks, and to everyone's disbelief, he found it. He had stayed at school a year longer than most and he was presentable and spoke well, and he drove a car. He was employed on the smallest retaining wage, the rest being commission, to travel four or five counties selling light fittings, shades and lamps and ornamental pendants, to smart stores, with a cheap range for small ironmongers. He still had his shiny wedding suit and collar, and best shoes. They came out and Miriam dabbed over them with white spirit whose fumes made her boys sick. But the suit came up well. Boxes of samples were delivered and had to be locked into the car out of reach of the boys. He left and did not know when he would be back, and Miriam settled into her chair and closed her eyes, as the sound of the engine died away, and felt peace and a sense of safety, having herself to herself. Michael and Clive were at school, Arthur George played in the yard all day, and Neville was a sleeper, a huge, bald, easily satisfied baby.

Perhaps that could be the last of it, somehow, she thought, and because the sun was shining that morning, stood on a chair to unhook the kitchen curtains and set them in a sink full of soapy water. It turned greasy grey after a few minutes. She was glad no one else was there to see it, her mother, who would have remarked, and Eve who kept a neat, clean house and would notice but say nothing. Eve's silence was the worst. Miriam had always, and quite without reason, felt harshly judged by her sister.

Later, she took Neville out in his pram, Arthur George sitting on the front, and by then the sun had long gone and the streets were darkened under heavy cloud. The whole town felt like a place struck down by some terrible affliction or contagious disease. No one smiled. People kept their eyes down and no longer made jokes to one another. Men hung about.

For the first time in her life, because of having a man with a car and work, Miriam felt superior. He came home every three weeks, sometimes looking downcast, having sold very little, once or twice buoyant, having taken orders. His pay was poor and the commission from the good weeks took a long time to reach him so that money was even more of a struggle and twice Miriam had to ask her mother to help out. Tommy came by and brought this or that, usually vegetables from the garden or a tin of cakes and biscuits Eve or he had made, and usually he left money in the teacup on the sideboard, saying nothing.

Miriam was alone with the boys and all of them asleep the night that the bangs came on the front door, waking her into a heart-pounding fright so that she was up and down without even a cardigan round her.

The door had been battered by Robbie Prentice, the six foot tall lad who lived with his family in Water Street.

Vera was dead, he said. His mother had heard a crash and then a silence so terrible she had got Robbie to break in.

'Go to Eve,' Miriam said, starting to shake. 'Have you called the doctor? Have you called the ambulance? Robbie, please will you go and fetch Eve? I've four children, I can't go.'

It was Tommy who came, of course, running all the way beside Robbie through the dark and going to the phone box to make the calls, arrange things, stay with Vera until the doctor was there. No one could have done anything. She had not died falling but had had a stroke as she was on the top landing and that had caused her to topple down the stairs.

It was the first time Miriam had had any experience of death and she shied away from it, not wanting to see her mother, using the children as an excuse.

But Eve went, leaving Jeannie Eliza next door, where Robbie carried her into the garden and swung her about and showed her the pigeons cooing softly in their loft. He said afterwards that she had gone quite still in his arms, her head to one side, listening.

Tommy went with Eve.

So that is death, she thought. Her mother looked

51

younger and somehow bland, all the character smoothed out of her face and as if she were an infinite distance away. She had always shown what she felt, anger or sadness, laughter and tears had been there for you to see. Now, she was expressionless. You could not read her.

Eve did not feel sorrow. She felt nothing. If she was to remember her mother, or to miss her, it would not be here or now.

The house had to be cleared, but the landlord was accommodating, they could take as long as they needed, he said, so that it was more than a week later that she and Miriam went together. Eve was there first, and opening the front door and hearing the silence, she felt her throat tighten, because her mother should have called out or come from the kitchen to greet her and she did not. There was a hollowness at the heart of it.

She wandered around, touching this or that, looking into her mother's bedroom at the white crocheted cover on the tightly made bed, and her own old room, almost bare because she had taken most things with her to her married home.

'Eve?'

'Up here.'

Miriam came up heavily, like an old woman climbing the stairs. She was expecting her fifth child now and because her muscles were slack as loosened ropes, showed further on than she was.

'What have you taken?'

'Taken? I've taken nothing.'

'There's plenty I could do with. What do you need?'

There seemed little enough in their old home to covet.

'I'd only like one or two bits of china,' Eve said. 'And the chiming clock.'

'You've a kitchen full of china.'

'Then have it. It doesn't matter, Miriam.'

The clock would be enough. The Westminster chimes had measured out her childhood and her growing up.

Miriam opened drawers and pulled things out, set them on the table, riffled through linen and spoons.

'There's the furniture,' Eve said, looking round. Neither of them had room for any of it.

'I want this table and the chairs in the front room. The boys have jumped ours to bits.'

Miriam ran her hand over the cold range. But that went with the house.

'John's been laid off,' she said. 'He wasn't getting the orders.'

Eve understood at last.

'Just the clock,' she said. 'You can sell up the rest. I've no need of any. You sell it, Miriam.'

9

S o that was death, she had thought, and remembered how she had felt so little, looking down at
her mother. Death. But of course then she had known
nothing.

It was late April, a cold spring and the plum blossom
barely out, the hedges not yet pricking green. Tommy
had whitewashed the kitchen and the paint smelled
damp and chalky. She had washed all her pieces of
china in the sink, with Jeannie Eliza standing beside
her on a chair and dabbing her fingers into the suds.

'We'll finish these off and go for a walk a little
way,' Eve had said and started to rinse and dry the
jugs and teacups, saucers and bowls, but Jeannie had
climbed down from the chair and wandered off into
the other room. When she went to fetch her, the child
was in Tommy's chair, curled asleep on the cushion.

Eve waited for an hour and then woke her, though by then the sky was curded with heavy grey cloud and they would not be able to walk far.

The china looked fine, gleaming even in the dull light. She wanted someone there to admire it with her. Tommy would but only if she drew his attention to it and then he would say, 'That looks grand,' just to please her.

She went to stir the child and saw that she was flushed. Her skin felt hot. Let her sleep then. Eve made tea. Rearranged the china again. Thought they would have baked potatoes with their cold meat that night.

Rain pattered against the window.

Jeannie did not wake until just before Tommy came in, soaked to the skin. He had to go and change clothes and brought the wet ones down to put on the airer in front of the range.

'She's not right,' Eve said.

'Colds. Everyone has them. It's so changeable.'

He knelt beside his daughter and touched her cheek. Frowned.

'Red hot.'

'Should I get her into her bed?'

'Sponge her with tepid water. It's not good to be so hot.'

Jeannie woke and her eyes were too bright. The heat came off her from a foot away.

'No,' she said, and tried to push her face into the cushion, turning it from the light.

At seven, Tommy went next door for Mary.

'Jeannie?' she said. But Jeannie cried out and pushed her head further into the cushion.

'She loves you,' Eve said, 'she doesn't mean it. She loves you, Mary.'

'Maybe get the doctor?'

Tommy stayed only long enough to put on his boots and waterproof. The rushing sound of the rain came into the house as he opened the door. Mary waited with Eve. They said nothing, only listened to the rain on the roof and the child's laboured breathing.

It was an hour, a hundred hours, a lifetime, of the rain drumming and the wind howling and the waiting, nothing said. Mary made tea. Jeannie turned her head restlessly and once or twice her limbs jerked in a sudden spasm, before she went limp and still again.

Eve sat looking at her. Jeannie was dark-haired and not very big for her age but she had never been ill other than having the usual infant teething problems. She was like Tommy, quiet but alert, and had a natural kindness about her that was his own mark. Now, the silken skin of her face seemed parchment-thin, although she was still flushed, and her eyes were sunken down. When she opened them it was as if she were confused, not knowing where she was but clutching at Eve's hand and for a second gripping it, before she lost strength again. Her eyebrows were fair, hardly there against the skin but her nose was already defined and her mouth wide. It had been possible from the day of her birth to see what she would look like later.

They had had joy of her from that first day and the joy had increased with every small change and growth, her look, her quietness, the way she watched them, the smile on the wide mouth, her laughter, which came only sometimes but when it did, pealed out so that Mary said she could hear it next door and that it made her laugh too.

Never since the day of her birth had Eve looked at her daughter in the way she did now, in a new amazement that she should exist at all and that she should have such miraculous beauty and be theirs, made of flesh and blood, skin and bone, and so infinitely precious. She did not know if the child was in pain but certainly she was in distress and if she could have taken that on herself she would have done so in an instant. What could be eased for her by the doctor or, if she was sent there, by the hospital, she had no idea, but that it would be done she did not doubt. It was the waiting that ate into her, the waiting, the helplessness, the lack of knowledge or skill to do more than touch and speak softly.

They came in the doctor's car, Tommy running into the house first, his face full of fear.

The doctor was gentle, careful, touching and listening, murmuring to Jeannie but otherwise offering no word.

The Westminster clock chimed the hour.

He got up at last and stood looking down at the child. 'She should be in hospital, but I don't like to move her. She's very ill.'

'What's wrong? Has she caught something? What's to happen to her? Can you . . .?'

Eve's words came out anyhow and left her breathless.

He shook his head. 'She has no rash on her skin. She could have a brain fever or it may be measles, and if that is the case the rash will come out.'

'Doesn't that help? I heard it brings about a crisis and then the fever goes down, isn't that true?'

He shook his head, not as if disagreeing with her but as if he did not know.

'You should take her to bed and shade the light. It plainly hurts her eyes. And have a sponge with tepid water and wipe her down, let her cool. I'll give you some powders to put on her tongue with a dab of sugar. And if she worsens, you come back for me.' He looked at Tommy.

'You mean if the fever doesn't ease?'

'If she seems in pain – if she has a fit, if her head seems to be aching, if she goes limp, or loses consciousness, if her eyes roll back into her head. And if she's still burning hot after the sponging and the powders. Then we will have to take her. But I would rather not.'

Eve coaxed open the child's mouth and sprinkled the powder and sugar on her tongue. She coughed once or twice but took a spoon of warm water and then turned her head away.

'I can't leave her on her own.'

So Tommy brought the cot into the front bedroom, before carrying Jeannie up the stairs with great tenderness, cradling her head against him and moving slowly. By the time she was undressed it was clear that her fever was lessening. Her face was still flushed but there was no longer so much heat radiating from her.

They did not turn on the lamp but left the door ajar and the landing light on. Eve did not leave her but lay on their bed, her arm outstretched to touch her daughter's damp hair that was pressed down onto her forehead. Tommy brought her tea and would have made food but she told him to eat it, for she could not.

And so the evening wore away and the night drew in and, eventually, they slept, Jeannie now cooler, her limbs no longer going into spasm, her head flat on the bed, as if she did not need to press it into the pillow.

An owl hooted softly from the far edge of the field.

Several times Eve woke and at once leaned over and looked carefully in the dim light to check on the child, but each time she saw and felt that she was sleeping peacefully, her breathing easier, her skin normal to the touch. Tears came with the relief and then she slept herself.

The mornings were light by six now and Eve woke as the dawn seeped through the thin bedroom curtains. She could hear Tommy moving quietly about in the kitchen, the rumble of the coal as he filled up the range, the sound of the water running into the kettle. She leaned out of bed and reached to the cot and knew.

These things happened, the doctor said, and there was no telling how or why. They happened. But his face was grey and he seemed suddenly older as he stood in the room, looking down.

'If I could have known . . . But I could not. You understand that, don't you? It seemed the greater risk to move her in the state she was, all the way to hospital. I would do the same today, you know. I'd have left her here at home.'

'At home to die,' Eve said. But she did not blame him. She understood, looking at his face, how it must be for him.

'Children die,' he said quietly. 'They do.'

'But if I –'

He shook his head. 'No. Not you, nor me. No way of knowing, no way of preventing it.' He did not look at her. 'The worst of all,' he said.

But for her the worst thing was that she wanted to explain to Jeannie and could not.

That week was the most terrible of Eve's life and the year that came after it the most terrible of years. She did not want the funeral to be public and open to all eyes, nor in the granite-grey town church and so Tommy arranged that it would not be, found out about St Paul-Alone and how they could take her there. No one came. Tommy himself carried her to the grave.

After that, life went on, a long, narrow, bleak tunnel through which they had to walk, one which would surely never end in any light. The only thing Eve had with which to comfort herself was that she had enjoyed every last moment of the little girl's life, and never once felt her to be a burden, difficult or tiresome, never once failed to love her absolutely, in flesh and spirit. She had been a happy, open, giving

61

child and loved easily in return, and no moment had been missed, no day wasted. She wished Jeannie back but regretted nothing.

Miriam had six boys and did not come to see them though she sent a brief letter. But Eve would not go to the town and besides, Miriam would never welcome her.

No other child was born to them. Tommy became quieter still, afraid to intrude on Eve's sadness. He felt the death of Jeannnie Eliza more than he had words to express – if he had had need of words. But neither of them did and the comfort was that they understood one another.

So great a pall lay over the town still that their grief would have simply added to it, been noted but after that absorbed into the misery of everyone's daily hardship.

It was easier at 6 The Cottages and Tommy was still in work. Jeannie's death had made no difference to any of that. Eve went through the spring and summer tending the garden and walking across the track to the peak and then up to St Paul-Alone, carrying flowers or a branch of fresh blossom and greenery to the grave. She could stand or kneel beside it half the day and never want to leave.

Tommy did not come with her. He said nothing but she knew that the sight of the grave and later, of Jeannie Eliza's name on the headstone was unbearable to him.

Eve did not bother to look at her own face closely in the glass when she brushed and put up her hair, but she knew instinctively that it had changed, that Jeannie's death was written there and had aged her.

Sometimes, going into a room or up the stairs, she had the sense that the child was there, pattering behind her but she never glanced over her shoulder. There was no need.

10

I T WOULD have been no wonder if one or other of
them had fallen ill that winter, for grief takes its
toll, but Eve was well, though the days were tunnels
to be trudged through, one leading to the next without
respite or purpose.

But one morning, catching Tommy's face as he
turned, she saw that there was something wrong,
though she could not then have said what it was or
how she knew. Something. That was all.

She waited. He worked steadily, walking or cycling
to the town and back, helped her with the jobs as
always, though he left in the dark and came home in
it, so there was nothing to be done outside. But the
fact that he sat across the table or in the armchair
opposite her meant that she could watch him more
closely and see the small changes. His face was thinner,

the bones became prominent as blades through his flesh. His clothes hung more loosely. He pulled his belt in one then another then another notch. But he still ate well, worked, slept, as usual.

Eve said nothing. Watched.

They did not talk about Jeannie Eliza because there was no need, she was with them, between them, all about them, and their love did not change or their grief lessen, though it might have dropped out of sight.

Christmas. 'Let us just not have a Christmas,' Eve said, for the memories were burned into her and there seemed nothing to celebrate. But Tommy said they should never ignore the day, that it would be selfish, and how would it help for them to pretend? So they killed a chicken and Eve made a small pudding and Tommy fetched a tree. On the previous year they had taken gifts and a large Christmas cake to Miriam and this year, he said, they must do the same. The boys should not be made to suffer. Gradually, then, they worked their way through the preparations and her heart lightened as she baked and wrapped and tried to think only of Miriam's sons. But that was not possible.

'Tommy looks poorly,' Miriam said, 'he looks a bad colour.'

The boys were thundering about, so much bigger now, taking up so much more room and air in the house, like clumsy animals. Arthur George had a thick livid scar on his forehead where he had fallen against the table edge and had to be stitched.

They ate tea, bread and butter and biscuits and some of the cake, though Tommy refused. They had their own, he said, the boys would need all this one.

He was good with them, better than their own father, who sat about all day in misery, having neither work nor interest, and could not bestir himself to take them out or play any game. They pulled Tommy out into the street for football, but Eve saw that he tired and was quickly out of breath and as he came back into the house, saw too that his flesh had a sallow tinge and his eyes were darkly circled. She said nothing until Christmas Day was over and they were inside all the next day because of the high wind and sleet. It was bitterly cold. She had been to the market for the boys' presents and while there got material to make a frock and a couple of new aprons. She had not bothered before but Tommy had urged her. 'You have something nice. It's what you deserve, Eve,' and put his hand into his pocket to pay at once, and suggested they have new curtains in the kitchen too. But she could not face changing anything in the house yet. The curtains were the ones Jeannie had known and sometimes pointed to for their brightness.

He had been eating less than usual, she was aware of that, scraping the leftovers from his plates into the bin. She made smaller portions, though not so much that he might complain, but even these he did not finish.

That same night, she went out into the scullery and found him putting fresh notches in his belt with the awl.

'You work too hard. You need to eat well.'

'Look at you, Eve,' he said, 'how thin you got. The weight dropped off you after . . . it's maybe just catching up with me.'

She shook her head. 'What should I tempt you with? The eggs are so good just now and I'll put more than a scrape of butter on your bread. Bread and top milk, that's what the old women swear by, with a sprinkling of brown sugar.'

But Tommy only laughed, threading his belt back through his trousers.

Still, over the following weeks, he grew worse.

He never talked about Jeannie, but one night he said, before putting out the lamp, 'I miss the little sounds she made through her sleep. I sometimes wake and think I'm hearing them.'

She reached out her hand and rested it on his arm.

'You're bone,' she said then, feeling along, 'just bone. You should see the doctor, Tom.'

'No, no. We don't need to spend money that way. Maybe you can make the bread and milk and sugar? That will soon set me up again.'

So she made it. She beat up two fresh eggs with milk and poured it over the buttered bread and got brown sugar specially. Every night before he went to bed he ate it slowly from one of the white bowls and told her it was good, even for invalid food. But she noticed that he scraped it round with the spoon until the china gleamed clean. It gave her pleasure to watch and she thought how strange it was, that she had had heart for nothing since Jeannie Eliza, but only gone heavily through the days, and now her heart should lift to watch him eat a bowl of bread and milk.

The weather turned warm and the leaves fanned out on the trees almost overnight. The swallows returned to nest above the door and the martins under the eaves. She saw Jeannie, pointing up to the skimming birds.

Tommy grew steadily worse. One morning, taking him a cup of tea, before he could be up first to fetch hers, Eve noticed a swelling just beside his jaw which seemed to have blown up overnight like a boil. She said nothing, just touched it gently with her finger. It was shiny-smooth and firm but there was no core or redness like any abscess.

He drank the tea carefully on the other side of his mouth and when he got up, said only, 'I'll be a bit later then, Eve, if I'm to take this for the doctor to look at.'

She almost told him to tell the doctor about everything else, the weakness and the fact that he was barely eating any food and the way he had to keep punching new notches into his belt, but she did not. He would say, or else the doctor would notice for himself and as one visit cost what it cost no matter how many things you took in to the surgery to be sorted out, Tommy would make the best use of it. But she watched him dress slowly and had to urge him to eat a small spoonful of porridge, a few scraps of bacon, before he set off, going without his old energy down the path and out of sight, his head bent, shoulders stooped, where they had always been straight and his step springing.

She filled the sink with suds and then stood, hands in the warm water to her wrists. She had lost Jeannie. Now she was to lose him. She had little doubt about it, having watched the life seep out of him over the past months, and she put it down to the death of the child, after which he had seemed to shrink into himself and lose heart for anything, though he had always tried to encourage her not to do the same but to enjoy what she could for Jeannie's sake, and remember her with gladness. Neither of them needed words, each knew well enough what was in the other's heart and neither could forget or hold out any hope for the future. She would have liked another child but sensed that there would not be one. That was for Miriam. All they could do was fill the quiet house with her boys from time to time, bringing some noise and life to it that way. But it was not the same. Jeannie had been a quiet, watching child.

Eve took her hands out of the suds and held them up and the soft iridescent bubbles slid down her wrists and back into the water as she watched and thought about Tommy, trudging into town and to work, and then across the town to the doctor and then back home, and wondered how he would have the energy in him.

I I

KNOWING BETTER than anyone how things were in the town, Dr McElvey had a surgery every evening at six for those who could not pay and those surgeries were packed to the doors and out of the doors, with men coughing and women white and stooped and underweight, rickety children and infants too lacking in energy to cry. He was never done until nine and then opened the windows wide to let out the smell of sick human beings and of misery and poverty and distress.

Tommy was among the first, finishing as he did at five and going straight down, though the room was starting to fill up even so, the benches round the walls taking as many as could be fitted onto them pushed up together. No one spoke, though many knew one another well enough, out of pride and a respect for each other's privacy, and out of the need to conserve energy, which talking drained too readily. People stared at the floor or the wall or fussed over their children and did not meet anyone else's eye, though when the door opened to admit yet another there was a quick glance and then glance away as the identity of the newcomer was noted. Tommy was known to several so that the eyes were on him as he walked in and to one, who had not seen him for some time, his thinness and the deep hollows of his face and his poor colour were a shock and it was all the woman could do to keep from staring. She would say later, at home and to the street, that Tommy Carr had the look of death upon him, and so word would spread.

He had brought an evening paper and held it up high so that the swelling in his jaw could not be inspected.

And if he had been in the street and heard what was said, that he had the look of death upon him, he would only have agreed because that was what was happening to him surely, the slow sideways movements of death towards him, the gradual tightening of its grip. But in the last week or two not so very slow at all.

He waited not more than half an hour and felt the eyes on his back as his turn came and he went in and the unspoken collective desire to follow him through

72

the door into the surgery, to hear and have suspicions confirmed. But the door was a heavy one and there was a curtain across the corner where the couch was.

Dr McElvey watched him come into the room, taking in the thinness and the slight stoop, the candle colour of Tommy's skin and the gleam of the swelling above his jaw, the expression in his eyes. He remembered Jeannie Eliza. He had not seen either parent since the child's illness and death but he was not surprised at the way the father looked now. A shocking death could have all manner of repercussions – or none. He had known families where a terrible death had occurred and other than the immediate tears and mourning, there had been no apparent effect on anyone, life had simply continued, though who knew what dark currents ran deep below the surface. But he saw the opposite too, and that almost every week, in a sudden death from heart failure, a suicide, a fit of madness, a series of infections that became progressively more serious until they overwhelmed their victim, who had been left with no more strength or inner resource to fight them and perhaps did not even wish to survive. Or there was this – the way Tommy Carr looked now.

He asked questions first, sitting calmly with his notepad and pen, glancing at the man every so often to try to gauge his reactions, read his mind. Eating, drinking, sleeping. Tiredness. Pain. Discomfort. Aching. Head. Neck. Throat. Chest. Breathing. Stomach. Bowels. Bladder. Limbs. And then the feelings. Sadness. Grief. Melancholy. Pessimism. Fears. Nightmares. Hallucinations. Changes of mood.

Tommy replied quietly, readily, and his face remained expressionless, until Jeannie Eliza was mentioned and then the physician saw the pain in his eyes, the stabbing of memory, the grief which was no age at all but fresh as yesterday.

'If you would slip out of your things and lie on the couch, I'll take a look at you, Tommy.'

He left the swelling beneath the man's jaw until last, concentrating on the emaciated body, feeling soft tissue and bone, pressing gently, his hands seeking out here and there, what he expected to find, and finding it.

'Now then, this swelling here.' He touched the lump with a forefinger, traced it lightly along. The skin was taut, the swelling firm.

'You can get dressed now. Thank you.'

Tommy had not spoken or made any movement other than to wince once or twice.

'I think you must have had indigestion for a while, Tommy.'

Tommy looked straight into the doctor's eyes, each man reading the other clearly there.

'Just a little while after eating.'

'But now?'

'Maybe a bit more . . . In the night I've felt it. I shouldn't eat toasted cheese before I go up to bed.'

Neither of them smiled.

'Do you get much relief from it?'

'I took bicarbonate of soda in milk a time or two, that helps a bit.'

'Harsh on the stomach lining though it is.'

Tommy did not answer and for a few moments the doctor looked at his notepad, pen in hand, working out what to say, how to say, whether to say. He set the pen down and leaned back, resting the tips of his fingers together. Watching him, Tommy remembered how he had been with the child, his tenderness and the way he had stood silently looking down at her, looking for some hope and finding none.

'I'm going to give you a mixture to settle your stomach and a bottle of tablets to help with your sleeping. And something for any pain you may have.'

'Will the swelling go down here?' Tommy touched his face.

'Give it a while. Give it time.' Dr McElvey got up and went over to the far corner by the window where the shelves and cupboards held the pharmacy, and washed his hands in the basin.

'I don't have a lot of difficulty in sleeping,' Tommy

said, 'so maybe just the medicine to settle my stomach? If I wake, I can make a cup of tea, you know.'

What he was saying, as the doctor knew, was that every bottle and pot and box full of this or that added to the cost.

'I won't give you many,' he said. 'You may find you're glad of them.'

When he handed the medicines over he said, 'If things worsen, we may have to get you looked at in hospital, Tommy. They've more tricks up their sleeve than I have.'

'I'll be right as rain.'

'And if you need me . . .'

The waiting room was packed now, with half a dozen men standing and more coming through the door. He slipped out without catching anyone's eye, the medicines in his jacket pocket.

Dr McElvey did not call the next patient at once, though he had seen the rows there were, patiently waiting. He stood looking through the net curtain of the surgery window onto the street and at Tommy Carr walking down it, shoulders hunched.

How long would it be? A month or less? The cancer was a great mass inside his gut, eating what was left of him away and there was precious little to go. He would not send him into hospital unless he must. There was nothing to be done, no tricks up their sleeve, and who in their right minds would want to go there to die? He was better off at home with the view to the peak out of the window and his wife to tend him.

He glanced at the notes. Thirty-one years old and looking seventy now. But out there, among those who coughed and ached and grew as thin as Tommy, there were plenty of the young looking old and the old with even less time to live.

Dr McElvey opened the surgery door and called for the next of them.

Tommy walked more slowly home than he had ever done and as she watched him from the window Eve had a piercing moment of fear that he would not make the journey again and then she realised a truth she had never before understood. Everyone has a time when they are in their prime of life. Everyone has as little as one year when they are the best they will ever be, the healthiest, strongest, most handsome, most full of energy and hope, when they might do anything and it can be seen upon them, this prime, in their eyes, on their skin, in their walk. But they do not know it. Perhaps they cannot know it. If they could they would not wish the time away, as people do, even children when they are unhappy or sick or trailing through some tedium of growing up. No one can know it about themselves but others may know. Others can see it on them and envy them. But it may even pass them by and then it is over and can never be recalled. And years later, they look back and know, recognise it as having been their prime, but of course by then it has gone and cannot be recalled.

Tommy had had his prime, she had had hers. Not Jeannie Eliza. When she had met Tommy Carr that had not been the time, it had come a little later, after they had moved into number 6 The Cottages. The year they had made things as they ought to be and he had gone striding off early every morning and back at night as if the distance were nothing at all.

And now it had gone.

He came in wearily and she helped him off with his coat.

'I thought you might have been later,' Eve said, putting the teapot down. Nothing more. He would talk in his own time.

He sat at the table sipping the tea and there seemed to be barely a flicker of life in him, but after a time, he reached into the pocket of his jacket and took out the medicines.

Eve felt a spurt of relief, as if there, in the golden-coloured liquid and the small box, was the answer to everything, to the pain in his stomach and weakness, his poor colour and lack of appetite, his thinness.

'He spoke of the hospital,' Tommy said, 'but he would rather me stay at home. I was glad of that.'

'Why would he think of the hospital at all?'

'Perhaps they'd find something.' He touched the medicines. 'I won't go.' He reached out his hand and touched hers briefly. 'Don't worry. Eve.'

He ate two spoonfuls of a thick stew she had made and a square of bread before he said he was too full to manage much, sounding apologetic, as he always was for not taking more after the trouble she went to, and then he read the label of the bottle carefully before taking some of the liquid in water.

'I'm going to do the chickens,' Eve said.

He came with her, though not all of the way to the bottom of the garden where the run was, and then stood watching. The rabbits had gone and they would not be replaced.

As they went back into the lighted kitchen, Tommy said, 'I wish she was here still.'

Eve was silent.

'I don't want to think of you being on your own.'

'I'm not on my own, I won't be, I've you. What are you saying?'

His expression as he turned to look at her was infinitely gentle, infinitely sad.

'Well, maybe for a while longer, Eve, maybe with the medicines . . . he didn't seem too sure.'

'Sure of what? How? Tell me.'

But he only shook his head and made for the stairs and she watched him climb as if he had weights tied to his legs and his body had turned to stone and the tears ran down her face for the sadness of it.

The next morning he left for work as usual though she did not know how he got down the stairs. He drank a mug of tea but ate nothing and it was painful to see him draw his jacket on as if every movement were an effort so great he might never finish making it. But he left.

Eve could not bear to watch him go but turned away from the window and tidied the dresser until she knew that he would be out of sight.

It was not usual for her to feel that she did not dare to be alone, but this morning she washed the pots quickly and went to the Ankerbys, not only because she was worrying about Tommy but because, suddenly, alone in the house meant alone. Jeannie Eliza, who had been there, always just behind or just ahead of her, always just out of sight but laughing somewhere, and calling out, ever since the day she died – Jeannie Eliza had gone. There was no child. No footsteps. No cry. No sudden laughter.

'Ah, my dear.' Mary Ankerby put out her hand and touched Eve's cheek the moment she saw her, and pulled back a chair for her and set the kettle on. Bert looked at her, shaking his head, and touched her shoulder, before going out of the door and into the garden.

'He went to the doctor,' Eve said.

Mary waited

'He got some sort of medicine. For the pain in his stomach and to help him sleep. But they don't seem to have done much for him.'

Mary Ankerby sighed. 'And the price of the doctors,' she said.

'He's very kind. That doctor. He came when . . . he was very kind.'

'I've watched Tommy.' Mary poured the tea out. 'He goes so slowly.'

'He doesn't complain at all but I hear him some-times, he makes a little moaning noise and puts his hand on his belly.'

They sat in silence after that, watching the sun move round, until Bert came back in and sat with them and the sun moved further, touched the scarlet petals of the geraniums on the sill and turned them to fire.

A little after that, Tommy passed by the window, half bent over and his walk so slow he seemed hardly to move at all.

12

Nothing was said between them but Eve knew, as Tommy did, that he would not go to work again. She also knew that he felt shame at being sent home. It was a fine, warm day and she put the garden chair out for him. He rested there for an hour or two, dozing, refusing anything to eat but asking her to bring him the medicine a couple of times. She stayed with him, hoeing and weeding, snipping the edges of the grass, collecting the eggs, things she thought would not worry him.

But in the early afternoon, the sound of a car coming down the track woke him from sleep, and he started to struggle up as John Bullard came through the gate.

'It's all right.' Eve laid her hand on his shoulder. 'Tommy hasn't felt so well,' she said, hearing the defiance in her own voice.

But John Bullard barely glanced. 'You need to come,' he said to Eve. 'Miriam's bad. She said to fetch you right away.'

'What's wrong?'

He shrugged. 'Only she can't manage with all of them.'

'And I have a sick husband, John. I can't just leave him.'

He stood staring at the ground.

'You should go, Eve,' Tommy said. 'Go to your sister. I'm fine, I'm just sitting here a bit but I'll go inside in a while, there's a few things I'll do.'

'You can't do anything, you have to rest. The doctor said that.' She swung round to John Bullard. 'Why can't you help her? It's your wife, your children.'

But he seemed like a tree, rooted to the ground, and did not look at her.

Eve sighed.

In the end, she went next door and Mary and Bert said they would be with Tommy, one or the other of them, and he could call for them, Bert would be in their garden and he could keep an ear out. Of course he would, Eve knew that, knew that Mary would fuss over Tommy, trying to coax him to eat or drink or lie down, that he would be as safe and comfortable with them as with her. But they were not her and she did not want to go.

'Only an hour, a couple of hours maybe, not more, John, I can't leave Tommy long.'

But her brother-in-law said nothing, merely turned and went towards the gate.

She was angry. She wanted to say angry things to him as they drove into the town and her anger surged inside her like things bubbling in a pot whose lid was clamped down. She stayed silent, thinking only about Tommy and her fears for him and for herself. He was dying, she had so little time left with him, she knew that, though she pushed the thought away, and now her sister was stealing some of that time from them.

As they drew up outside the house, Eve said, 'I can't leave Tommy long. You have to understand.'

John Bullard shrugged and went ahead.

The place was a tip. It smelled sour and the hall and the kitchen were a mess of unwashed dishes and pans, toys and a sinkful of nappies, bottles of milk gone curdled and old cat dishes crusted with dried meat.

The boys came streaming out to her and clutched her round the legs and pulled at her hands, six of them now, and looking ragged and grubby as street children. Eve felt ashamed, though not of them – for them she felt only love and a weary sympathy. But she was ashamed to have a sister leave her own boys to such a mess and of John Bullard, who sat down in the chair but pushed the youngest child away from him as he did so.

'Where is she?'

'In bed. That's where she's stayed since it happened. She ought to be feeling more like rousing herself now.'

'And you . . . you put the kettle on and make some tea and cut some bread. They look as if they haven't had anything to eat.'

Eve went out, picking up the youngest as she did so, and climbed the stairs with him. He pushed his face into her shoulder and she stroked his rough, dirty hair.

Miriam was curled on her side but awake. The little one struggled to go to her, but seeing him, she turned away.

Eve opened the window wide.

'What's the matter?'

'I'll be all right.'

'You have to tell me why you're in bed. I shouldn't have left Tommy, he's very ill.'

'There's no one else can take care of them. He doesn't bother.'

'No, he does not and he'll find he has to start. I

have to get back home, Miriam, I can't take your place again.'

'It won't be long. A day or two, but it leaves you so weak.'

'What? What leaves you weak?'

She knew how angry she sounded. Miriam had almost never heard her raise her voice.

'I miscarried,' Miriam said. 'He didn't even bother to tell you that much.'

'Oh, Miriam.' Eve set the baby on the floor.

'It's happened before. It just leaves you weak.'

Eve sat on the bed. Her sister was pale, her skin dull, her hair lank.

'I'm sorry,' she said. 'It must be hard. But it will make you ill, Miriam, it will wear you out, all this.'

'It already has.' Her voice was as dull as her skin and flat as her hair.

'Can't the doctor . . .?' But she didn't bother to finish.

'I'll clear up and sort out the boys,' she said. 'I'll make them something to eat for tonight. But he'll have to see to them after that. I can't stay. I'm sorry but I can't.'

'What's the matter with Tommy?'

He is dying, Eve wanted to say, to shout out. He has a growth in his stomach and another on his neck, he is in pain, he can't eat, he weighs nothing, he can hardly stand. He is dying.

She felt the baby's small hands round her leg, and the weight of him trying to pull himself up. She bent down and lifted him and he tried to launch himself onto the bed and his mother.

'Oh, don't put him on me, I can't do with him now,' Miriam said. 'I can't do with any of them.' And she turned onto her other side, away from the baby, not so much as glancing at him.

Eve cradled his head close to her and took him out of the room.

Mary went into 6 The Cottages every hour and each time it seemed that Tommy had slipped a little further down, a little further away from her and from this world, though he smiled and raised his hand and, once, sipped some milk. Later, Bert helped him up the stairs to bed, half carried him he was so weak, and helped him undress too with gentleness and a respect that Tommy was aware of and grateful for. But it was Eve he wanted. Eve could not make the pain easier but her presence helped him bear it quite well.

'She should be here,' Mary said in the late afternoon.

'She knows,' Bert answered. 'She was torn.'

'That sister.'

'What could she do?'

Mary shook her head and went back to Tommy. She listened at the foot of the stairs to the silence and for a moment her heart jumped, but then she heard a slight sound and went up. She saw his eyes, wide open and looking at her, and with small pin points of pain in their centres. His forehead was damp and she found a clean handkerchief to wipe it gently.

'Eve?'

'She'll be home any minute now.'

Tommy smiled and closed his eyes, reached for Mary's hand and held it with what grip he could find in him. She saw that he had very little strength left.

'Eve.'

'You have to go for her,' she said. Bert stood up at once, seeing the expression on her face and what it meant.

'Quick as I can.' Though he was an old man and quick was not so very quick now.

'Get that lummock to bring you both back in his car.'

His fingers seemed twice their usual thickness as he tried to lace his boots quickly. When he had set off, Mary returned next door and sat at Tommy's bedside, praying for Eve to get back in time. But Tommy seemed a little easier, sleeping quietly.

Mary put her own hand over his and held it there.

* * *

Eve fed the children on what she managed to find and washed them as well as she could, though the water was barely warm because Miriam did the range and John had no notion how until Eve showed him, pinching her lips tight together so that she would say nothing angry, apportion no blame. It was not for her to criticise him out loud. He watched her sullenly and she wondered how much notice he took or whether he had any intention of doing it for himself after she had left. No, he would wait for Miriam, whine until she got up before she was ready and have her riddle out the ashes and heft the coal into the range.

'I might take a walk out,' John Bullard said.

'And you might not. I can't stay, I told you, John, I'm needed at home.'

'You're needed here.' He sat down in the chair again and picked up the paper.

She did not answer.

Upstairs, Miriam slept.

Bert Ankerby arrived breathless, his face contorted with the effort of walking so fast, for he was a man who had always moved at a slow, steady pace, which got things done fine, he said, and for a few moments he could say nothing but stood, the breaths heaving in his chest, so that Eve was afraid he might drop down dead. But after a moment, the breathing settled and he refused a chair to rest, simply saying, 'You have to come now, Eve.'

'What do I do about the boys?'

'They're all right, why shouldn't they be? I'm here, Miriam's upstairs.'

'No, John, you're taking us in your car.'

He started to protest, but seeing how it was, how even mild Bert Ankerby stood over him, and Eve's anger, he got up reluctantly.

'I'd better wake Miriam,' Eve said, 'tell her you'll be back as quick as you can. That the boys are on their own.'

'Leave her be,' John Bullard said, and she understood, that it happened often, the boys were used to being on their own and having to look out for one another and the baby between them.

John drove, Bert Ankerby sitting awkwardly in the back, his huge frame as if it were folded into a matchbox, Eve in the front and leaning forward to see the end of the town lights and the beginning of the darkness and the track that led to The Cottages and her dying husband.

13

Dr McElvey stood at the window of his study looking out at the same darkness, and thinking also of Tommy Carr, and as he did so, he heard the voice of the first physician he had worked with after qualifying, the man who had taught him more than anyone about sickness and health and the men, women and children whose lives they tended. He could hear his fine voice speaking into his own quiet room, speaking of the illnesses they all dreaded, the end they prayed not to come to and how they should be helped.

'Remember one thing – they dinnae want to ken, Ian. Nearly all of them, you can be sure, and it's your duty to spare them. *They dinnae want to ken.*'

And so he had discovered for himself. He wondered now if Tommy Carr had wanted to know or if he, like so many, had guessed for himself and yet, with a strange excess of fellow feeling, wanted to spare the doctor from understanding that. There had been a look in his eyes.

The growth had been large and growing, everything pointed to the tumour below the man's jaw as having seeded from it and there would be others eating away what was left of his body. There was no point in knowing how many or where.

Tommy Carr.

Dr McElvey went out of his study to find his wife.

Ten minutes later, he was driving to 6 The Cottages, obeying the inner voice he had been trained to listen to. It told him when someone needed him and why.

Tommy Carr.

It was some moments after he had knocked before Eve came to the door. He heard her footsteps on the stairs first. When she saw him her face, already pinched and grey with anxiety, flashed up a look of fear.

Dr McElvey took off his hat. 'I think perhaps you may need me to have a look at Tommy.'

She held the door, uncertain, and he knew well that it was the question of cost running through her mind, as it did through them all.

'Don't worry, Eve,' he said. 'It's all in with the same bill, you know, it's not an extra call.'

Though he knew full well that he had not yet sent

any bill, nor would until he was sure of Tommy, one way or the other.

'He's very ill, Doctor. He seems to have gone down just in the last hour or so. I don't know what's wrong.'

They dinnae want to ken. But did the wives and families?

'Let me take a look then,' he said.

She led the way, up the narrow stairs. 'Can I get you anything, Doctor?'

'No, no . . . I just need to make sure Tommy's comfortable. I've had him on my mind.'

As he looked at the man, lying with his knees up, as if it helped with the pain in his belly, he thought there was very little time and knew again that he had been right to obey the voice that prompted him.

'Tommy,' he said, putting his hand on the man's brow. It was cold and clammy. He touched his arm and his chest. Tommy shuddered.

'Cold.'

'I know. Shall I just take a look at your stomach?'

Tommy looked at him out of eyes that had sunk deep down but whose irises were a brilliant, vivid blue. McElvey had seen that sometimes too.

He touched the swelling on Tommy's neck. It was harder but not larger. He pulled the bedclothes down gently. The swelling in his stomach was huge, as if the man were with child. He gave a slight whimper.

'I can give you something to help now.'

'There's only a spoonful left of the medicine he brought back,' Eve said. 'It seemed as if it helped him just a little.'

'He needs something stronger to ease him now.'

'It won't harm him?'

He turned to look at her anxious face in the dimly lit room and looking, remembered the death of Jeannie Eliza. So this was the next blow she had to bear.

'No, Eve. It will ease him and help him sleep. Nothing more.' He set his bag on the dressing table and hesitated, wondering whether he should draw up a syringe or simply give a greater strength by tablet.

Tommy made a sound and started trying to sit up but could not. Eve wiped his brow with a clean folded handkerchief.

'Try and keep him covered. He'll feel cold.'

He counted a dozen tablets into the box. 'He should have two of these soon, when he can drink them down. He should sleep then.'

He looked at Eve and saw the unspoken question on her face.

'You try to rest yourself now.'

She led him down the stairs but at the door she turned. 'Is there nothing you can do for him? Can nobody?'

'Ah, Eve. You can do the most, you know that. Being with him, making sure he's comfortable. That'll be all he wants, to have you with him.'

'It's hard.'

'It is.'

'And harder knowing . . .'

He waited, but she shook her head and lifted the latch to open the door. It was raining a little on the breeze.

'I'll come by tomorrow.' Dr McElvey touched her arm.

He would, but whether to see Tommy Carr alive again was another matter.

14

NIGHT CAME. Tommy lay quietly except that he groaned once or twice and once cried out suddenly when he tried to turn over. Eve got a second blanket and laid it over him, but his hands and face felt cold to the touch and now and again he shivered violently.

He took the tablets, sipping the water from the cup she held close to his mouth. His skin was dry and thin as tissue.

But a little while afterwards he slept and then she lay down beside him, though still dressed, and reached out to touch his hand for comfort. Cold. There was no moon and she had left the window a little open so that the curtain moved occasionally and she could smell the damp earth and the rain on the wind.

What would she do? Would she stay here? She could

not think of herself being anywhere else, could not bear it, but it was Tommy's wage that paid the rent. Well then, she would have to work, though where or at what she had no idea. There were few jobs and she had no skills or none that anyone would pay much for.

She caught herself. 'I am thinking as if he were dead. He is not dead.'

But it would not be long. It could not be.

And then she slept, lightly, but it helped her and she did not dream, but was just aware of the curtain blowing and of Tommy's cold hand.

She woke because he had said something, and when she turned, she realised that he was sitting up.

'Tommy?'

'Oh, Eve, would you open the window?'

'It is open.'

'I'm so hot. Can you open it a little more? I feel I'm burning. I woke with it. It's as if you'd opened the lid of the range and set me beside it.'

She reached out to him and felt his skin, but even before she touched it she could feel the warmth coming off him.

She switched on the lamp, got out of bed and drew one curtain back, but she was afraid to let in more cool air in case he took a chill and pneumonia.

Now he had pushed back the bedclothes and unbuttoned his pyjama jacket.

'Tommy, try not to do that, you could catch a bad cold. Are you thirsty?'

'Maybe some water would help cool me? I was so cold before. I slept well, the pain was better.'

'Those tablets the doctor brought . . . he said they were stronger. That's good you slept so peacefully.'

'I *was* peaceful. That's the right word. I feel peaceful now. As if this warmth were going right through to my bones, right through my body – it's like sitting in the sun.'

Eve looked at him. There was something in his face, something about him that had changed. His face looked less ghostly, his eyes less sunken into his head and pain-filled.

She went down into the quiet kitchen and opened the back door and the soft sound of the rain on the grass was like a balm. She ran her hands under the cold water.

Perhaps this was what happened sometimes, nearer to death? The cold and then the sudden feeling of heat, the last alertness before the mind clouded again? She did not know. Death seemed to take so many forms. But if he had a little while of calm and ease she would be thankful for it. She drank a little of the water herself and it tasted of the spring from which it came up on the peak, cold and clear and sweet.

He took the beaker from her in steady hands and drank it slowly down to the last.

'Ah, Eve, that's the most wonderful drink I ever drank.'

His voice was so heartfelt that she laughed. 'It's only water.'

'I never tasted water like it.'

'Are you still so hot?'

'Not so much.'

'How's your stomach? Do you need any medicine again?'

He leaned forward a little. 'It's not painful now.'

'Those tablets must last a long time then. Only tell me if you need more.'

He lay down on his back. 'It was like being in the sun. The heat of it.'

'Maybe that was the tablets as well.'

'Maybe, but I know it's better being warm than cold.'

'How are you now?'

He paused, as if checking himself carefully. Then he said, 'Tired. As if I fought the war and all on my own.'

This time, she undressed before she lay down. She had been terrified that she might have to go and get

Bert to fetch the doctor, or bring Mary in to be with her, she had believed he would die at any minute, but as he seemed quieter, and his pain had eased for now, perhaps she could sleep better herself.

She switched off the lamp and reached to him again. His skin felt as it always used to feel.

'You were so hot I could have dried the washing by putting it by you,' she said.

'Yes. How long did it last, Eve? Feeling so warm.'

'I know it woke you and you were pushing the clothes off trying to get cooler. But I don't think it was long. Like a sudden fever.'

'And it burned itself out.'

'Yes,' she said. And remembered, as she knew that he remembered. But his illness and Jeannie Eliza's had been quite different.

She felt his body go heavy as sleep came over him and so, after a little while, she herself slept too, to the gentle patting of the rain and the soft movement of the curtain.

She slipped out of bed and downstairs before six. Tommy was very still.

The rain was over and the sky clear, but when she opened the door onto the garden and the first clucking sounds of the chickens, she could still smell the dampness on leaf and grass and earth and see how it had brought out the fresh green in everything. She filled the pan and took it down to the birds.

She liked this time alone and felt better for sleeping, but in her mind was only the worry of how Tommy would be when he woke, whether his pain would have come back and increased, whether he would again be cold as stone or burning hot. How much longer he would go on living. She had thought he would die the previous night and so did the doctor, she had told that from everything he had said, the look on him, the way he had touched her arm. How could you go on waiting for someone to die, knowing that they surely would, but not knowing when? How could any person?

It was so quiet when she went back into the house that rather than disturb Tommy's sleep she riddled out the range and filled it, set the kettle on and took one of the warm eggs she had just picked up from the straw and put it on to boil. She felt guilty, enjoying all of it, the quiet movements, the small sounds, the smell of the air coming through the open door, but she needed the time to gather her strength again, for who knew what was to come that day.

Upstairs, Tommy woke. For a moment, after he opened his eyes, he was troubled, sensing something different and strange and not understanding what it was. Eve had gone down. The house was quiet, but then he heard the sound of the spoon scraping against the tin and the hens clucking in their scramble for the food. He lay still. He had no pain. He felt quite at ease and when he moved, first his limbs and then his body, there was still no pain or even the discomfort he had grown used to over the past months. He put his hand up and touched his finger to the swelling under his neck which had been hard and giving him such pain to breathe and swallow, though he had said little about it to Eve, not wanting to worry her more. But Dr McElvey had felt it and known.

The swelling was no longer there. He had the wrong side, then, and moved his hand to the right but there had never been any swelling on the right and there was none now. Back again. Feel. Up. Down. Left. Right.

Nothing. His jaw and face and neck were as they had used to be, though he was rough for want of a shave.

Nothing.

He moved his hands down to his belly which had been swollen and which he had barely been able to touch, the pain of it had been so great. Now he felt nothing at all but his finger on the skin. One finger. Two. He traced them slowly across. Three and then the palm of his hand. He put the smallest amount of pressure he could, then a little more, and then more, until he was able to push down quite far. No pain. Nothing. His stomach was flat and smooth. As it had always been.

As it had been.

He sat up, bracing himself, as he had done for so long, against the immediate pain, but his body moved quite easily in the old way. He took a breath, then a deeper one, filled his lungs full, full, held his breath and let it go with a great explosion so that he gasped. But there was no pain.

He lay back and closed his eyes, not understanding any of it, and then he heard voices in the room below, Eve's quiet one and that of a man. Bert Ankerby must have come to see what he could do to help her with the heavy jobs, as he had been doing for the past week or more and which had made Tommy ashamed, for Bert was in his seventies and he himself a young man and always proud of his strength.

Footsteps on the stairs.

Dr McElvey sometimes lost sleep over a patient and he had lost most of the previous night worrying about Tommy Carr, anxious for him not to linger, concerned about the level of pain he would have to endure, angry that there was no more he could do for the man other than start to administer his medicine via injection and to give higher doses. Life was hard for everyone in this town now that this works and that had closed and there was no prospect of other employment, that men and women struggled on pence and tried and so often failed to retain some dignity, that children were born into houses where poverty and misery and dirt and sickness and hunger were the norm.

He did what he could and it was always too little and there were plenty of others in pain, the same pain as Tommy Carr or a different one, it scarcely mattered, and the hospital wards were crammed full. But because of Jeannie Eliza and because of something about the couple and about the home they had, out of the way and contented and calm, because of things he himself did not fully grasp, the doctor felt acutely for them and when he could no longer bear to lie trying and failing to sleep, he had come out to them early. As he drove towards 6 The Cottages, he was leaden-hearted, sure that he would find Tommy dead or near to death, dreading to look into Eve's face. He shocked himself. He was a doctor. He tried to cure and comfort his patients and to treat them kindly, but he had never become close to any one of them, never been touched deep in his own heart as he was touched now.

Eve was tending to the chickens.

'I woke so early. Tommy is asleep now. It's very good of you to come here again to us.'

He said nothing more about payment, not wanting to hurt her pride, but it would be on her mind, he knew. He tried to keep his charges modest, but he had been to the house and seen Tommy at the surgery, there were the medicines. She knew there had to be a bill she would struggle to pay.

'Can I pour you some tea, Doctor? I'm making fresh for myself. Tommy can't manage hot things. He finds it hard even to swallow cold water.'

'I'll go to him first and then a cup of tea would be very welcome, thank you. You stay here, finish your jobs. I know my way up, Eve.'

He went up and into the bedroom and stopped dead. The curtains were drawn back, the window open, and Tommy was standing beside it, both arms outstretched, head back, taking in lungfuls of air.

15

EVE LOOKED up. Her hands were shaking and her mind was a jumble of fears and bewilderment so that when she saw him she dropped a cup into the stone sink, smashing it. She flew out of the door, down the path.

'Tommy!'

But he was already at the gate.

'Tommy, what are you doing?'

Then he was through the gate and closing it. He wore his old trousers with the belt he had had to notch in so many times, and the jacket that hung off him like an old garment on a scarecrow.

'Let me be.'

'You can't . . . Where are you going?'

He looked at her, his face grave and kind and pale.

But his eyes were bright. The sunken look of the last weeks had quite gone.

'I'll be back in a while.'

She looked at him helplessly. 'Did the doctor –'

'The doctor said nothing. What was there to say?'

He smiled at her and turned away and Eve watched him walk steadily along the track, his stride careful, as if he was still not sure of his footing and whether his body would bear him. He did not look back. She watched him until he was way off, going towards the peak. It was a cool, grey morning and a thin cloud wreathed over it. She went to look at the chickens, bent to pull up a clump of dock leaves. Perhaps Bert or Mary was at one of the windows, watching her, watching Tommy, and as bewildered as she was. Was he bewildered himself? He had said almost nothing and Dr McElvey too, who had come down the stairs at last and slowly, his face furrowed, and gone out without a word other than 'Goodbye, Eve'.

She felt as if a door had been slammed in her face. Something strange or terrible had happened – for she could not think of it in any other way, at least not yet – something that had thrown her into a confusion so that she was unsure even of the ground beneath her feet. It was as though Tommy had wanted it hidden even from her.

She went in and saw the broken china in the sink and stared at it.

She doubted her own name.

Neither of them had slept. Tommy had not been able to lie still but had sat up, stood, paced about, gone down the stairs, and all the time, touching his hand to his stomach and then to his neck, his eyes huge, face pale.

She had asked what had happened over and over again and all he had said, once, was, 'I was hot. There was the heat, like a furnace.'

'But why should that take all the pain and swelling away? The medicine the doctor left –'

'No.' He spoke abruptly, as he had never done to her before. 'It hasn't to do with the medicine.'

She had not known what else to say. But when he had asked her to touch the swelling on the side of his jaw and to press her hand into his stomach she had done so. The swelling had gone, not leaving any shrunken skin or roughness, leaving nothing, as if it had never been there and his stomach was flat and smooth and the skin a healthy colour. When she had pressed and pressed even more firmly, he had not flinched.

'I don't understand what's happening.'

Tommy had not replied.

She had cooked and he had eaten, more than he had eaten for a long time, though not as much as he used to put away, and drunk four cups of tea. He had been withdrawn and silent, not exactly his old self nor yet the one she had grown used to and had to look after. She ate a little though she had no appetite.

More than anything, she longed for something to be familiar and to be able to get a grasp on life. More than anything, she was frightened.

She wondered now how she could face the Ankerbys, what she might say that would make sense, and she decided there was nothing and so she hid from them. Yet she wanted someone to be with her so that she did not have only her own thoughts for company, thoughts that led to a sort of madness, for what else was all of this but a madness? Tommy had been sick to death. He had had a vast tumour in his stomach, a swelling on his jaw, pain and sickness. He had been wasted and exhausted, he had been unable to eat or drink. She had prepared herself for his dying, yesterday, today, not wanted him to die, but somehow needing to accept that it would happen. She had been so unprepared for the death of Jeannie Eliza that the shock had scarred her for the rest of her days, but this time she had some warning.

But what would happen now? Was he well after all? Would he be ill again tomorrow or next week? Was he still going to die soon? She did not know what she was preparing for, if anything, if anything. She poured a glass of water and sat at the kitchen table, staring into it, not thinking, not feeling, just staring, while Tommy had gone walking across the track that led to the peak and she could not know if he would return.

She half thought of going to see Dr McElvey, for perhaps he would be able to explain it all to her, would have an understanding of what had happened. But even as she stood up and went to comb her hair and get into her coat, she knew she could not go because the doctor knew nothing, understood nothing, or why had he run from the house that morning, ducking his head for fear of having to confront her, say something?

She sat down again.

In the house next door, Mary Ankerby said again that something had happened, something was not right. Bert did not reply, for what could be said?

Between the two houses was a strange fog of silence and bewilderment and neither the Ankerbys nor Eve could bring themselves to try and reach one another through it.

16

Tommy walked. His body felt light. He could lift his feet without effort and he had no pain or even much sensation in him. He did not think, but only exulted in his own steady, even pace across the track towards the peak and round the base to the other side.

His clothes felt loose upon him. The air touched the skin of his face and was cool.

He knew where he was going but not why. Eve was the one who went there now and had understood why he did not, even before the illness, but his legs would have taken him there today if they had been tied together.

He expected to be alone but as he approached the last few yards leading to the church he saw that two women were there, going among the gravestones and peering at the inscriptions. Tommy stopped. He did not want to be pried upon, felt an odd shame for having come here, though he was angry at himself for there was no reason.

'Tommy Carr?'

He remembered her dimly, though not her name, a friend of his mother's from years back. She had sometimes come round.

He wanted to duck away but instead just went on standing until she came right up to him, a stout woman with a turn in her eye.

She stared into his face. 'It is Tommy.'

'It is.'

'Well.'

She called out, without turning her head. 'Come here, see who it is.'

He felt like one of the gravestones, being such an object of their attention. When the other woman approached, he knew her at once, Ivy Matlock, whose husband had been crushed by the steel beam coming loose from its winch and who had run all the way to the factory barefoot and screaming so that she had to be held back by three men, though she fought and even bit them.

'Ivy.'

'But you were dead – or at death's door with it standing right ajar, Tommy Carr.'

'And now look at you, walking out here.' The other one spoke as if she were accusing him of some failing or even of a crime.

'I'm fine,' he said, and then moved to go past them, but they were not having it and blocked his way. He wanted to shove them aside with an anger he had rarely known. If he had moved he would have knocked them both down.

'What, it was all lies then? And you perfectly fit?'

He did not have to explain anything to them and besides, he could not, he could not explain it to himself, yet he was stuttering something.

'People will say anything.'

'Why would I do that?' he asked, amazed that they should think it. Why would he?

And then they let him pass them, though he felt their eyes on his back like needles, and all the time he was walking slowly to the grave he knew they had not moved but only went on watching him.

Jeannie Eliza Carr
Aged 3 years
Beloved daughter

He touched the stone tenderly. The wind blew across the hill with the sweet smell of the land on it.

113

Whatever he had wanted to find, he found it then.

The strangeness and bewilderment and confusion fell away and he was left as if he had been rinsed in clear water. He remembered the child pattering behind him down the path, taking his hand and laughing, remembered not with sadness but with a strange feeling of rightness and content. He could not understand any of it, but now that seemed not to matter. What had happened to them both had happened and that was all.

Something fell into place but he did not know what or where.

Something righted itself that had been out of true but he did not know how.

Behind him, the two women spoke in low voices but he no longer minded them.

The wind moved the grass beside the child's grave.

In his surgery, the doctor attended to his patients diligently, listening, diagnosing, prescribing, bandaging, stitching, reassuring, and not one of them knew that his mind was elsewhere and not on them but on Tommy Carr. When the last woman and her children had trailed out into the street and he was tidying away the instruments and putting them in the steriliser, ordering the pharmacy shelves, setting the notes straight, he went over and over what he had seen, what had happened, and faced only bewilderment. He had no doubt at all that Tommy had been days or even hours from death, that he had had a cancer eating away his intestines and seeding itself throughout his body and bursting out in another swelling on his neck. No doubt. He would have gone to his grave without doubt, gone before the Coroner without doubt, been judged on his own certainty.

Yet the man he had seen early that morning had no tumours and though still thin and a little weak, was no longer a few breaths from his death.

Such things did not happen. He himself did not make such mistakes. He had known improvement, even cure with this terrible disease, but not like this because this was impossible.

It troubled him greatly. It undermined his confidence, in himself and in medicine. He felt as if he were trying to walk on shifting sands and sinking.

He had visits to make and then another surgery. By early afternoon he had begun to be sure that Tommy Carr would fall ill again and that the swellings would be as they had been and death pushing open the door. If he had not been sure of it, he fancied that he would have gone mad.

The sense of rightness and quiet stayed with Tommy as he walked steadily back from the churchyard, watched as far as they could see him by the two women, but quite unworried by that now.

He would make the tea for Eve, the first time he had been able to turn his hand to help her in the house for so long, and the next day he would be up and off to work early as always and perhaps there would be an end to it.

But when he reached the house he found it empty and silent. He took off his boots and called out but there was no one, until Eve came running to the back door, her face crumpled with anxiety.

'Oh,' she said, letting it out like a sigh, as if it had been pent up within her. 'Oh.'

And then, 'I was afraid you would never come back.'

'Why should you think it? Of course I came back.'

'I can't ask you to go out again but I must, I need to fetch the doctor to Mary. She's lying on the ground where Bert found her when he came in from the garden. He has to stay with her. I'll tell him you're back.'

Tommy followed her into 5 The Cottages. He saw Bert Ankerby first, his huge frame in the old flannel shirt bent over Mary, whose head flopped over to one side like a cloth doll, one leg bent.

'Mary,' Bert said. 'Come on, Mary. Come on, girl.'

Tommy went closer.

'Should we move her, lift her onto the settee, put

a cushion under her head?' Eve said. 'She's on the cold stone, it can't be right for her like that.'

'Mary, come on, girl.' Bert had one of her hands between his, chafing it. He looked up at Tommy but hardly seemed to see him.

Tommy bent down. He had seen death before and this was not death but she was pale as wax and very still.

'She's not one for fainting,' Bert said, his voice full of bewilderment. 'She's a strong one, Mary.'

'Should we try and lift her?' Eve said again.

'It might be best,' Tommy said. 'Lay her down more comfortably. She could come to harm there.'

He reached out his hand to touch Mary's arm, but as he did so, he almost pulled it sharply back, as if electricity had shot through him. He felt the current of it coming from his hand and passing to Mary.

They lifted her onto the couch and Bert fetched a woollen rug and draped it carefully over her.

She pushed it away, her eyes wide open, struggling to sit up.

'Mary,' Bert said. 'I said you were a strong one, Mary.'

'You'll make yourself faint,' Eve said. 'Put your head back again, Mary, you're not well.'

Tommy stood watching. He did not know what had happened to Mary Ankerby, but it seemed like a stroke or a fit and she had not been conscious, her face had been drained of blood. Bert said she had talked strangely, as if her words wouldn't come out right and then she had fallen and not moved or spoken again. 'I rubbed her hands and said her name only she couldn't hear me,' he said again and again now, 'she couldn't hear me.'

Mary lay back, a little colour coming into her face now, the woollen blanket on the floor.

'Shall I get you a drink of water, Mary?'

But Eve was already bringing it and sitting beside her to raise her head, help her drink.

Mary took almost half the cup and then looked around, as if the room were unfamiliar and she was trying to work out where she was, who they were.

'Should I still go for the doctor?'

'Who wants a doctor?' Mary asked. 'I had a turn, that's all. People have them. Why would I need a doctor for that?'

Eve looked round uncertainly.

But Tommy had gone, back to their own house, back, dragging himself as if he were filled with sand, slowly, slowly up the stairs and into the bedroom. Taking off his jacket and boots again was harder than a day's work, harder than any walk home in the face of a gale. He lay down and slept at once, an exhausted, drowning, dreamless sleep, and did not wake for nine hours.

17

WORD WENT round as word does, word of what had happened to Tommy Carr and of what Tommy Carr had done, though where the word first came from who could say. And word changed and grew extremities.

Dr McElvey was asked by a dozen patients a day about Tommy Carr and a dozen about Mary Ankerby, and word was passed to him as he went into houses and treated patients and listened and nodded but said nothing.

Tommy woke heavy-headed but still early and got up as he had always done, to riddle the ashes and fill the range and set the kettle on to boil.

'You surely can't be right to go back to work,' Eve said. But he smiled and tied his bootlaces and set off and as she watched him walk away she could hardly remember how it had been with him only a couple of days before. He looked as usual.

Mary, coming down the path with a tin of scraps for Eve's chickens, seemed quite as usual too, passing the tin across the fence, looking at the rain clouds building behind the peak, her face as bright as always. Eve could make no sense of it.

The staring began as he joined the rest of them walking in twos and fours towards the works. Nothing was said, a few nodded, and yet he could hear the whispers like smoke on the air. He felt as if he had committed some terrible crime and been found out, felt like a victim of the plague, felt like a leper among his old colleagues and friends. They moved slightly away. Tommy thought, they did that to witches.

But once in the works he could get on with the jobs in hand and the din of the machines meant no one could ask him questions. But they could still look and from time to time catch one another's eye. Yet over days they would have got used to him again and soon enough it would be forgotten, because there would be some other thing, as there always was, some death or birth or accident or shame.

At twelve thirty he went out to drink his can of tea

and eat the food he had packed for himself, and those who had gone at twelve returned to the din inside. He heard it but not first. Others who were on their way in heard it but the thud was muffled by the wooden doors. Then the doors opened and the shouting started, men and women, voices, names, cries for help. He rushed in with several others, dropping their food and running.

One of the twelve o'clocks had tripped and fallen and in falling, a pile of the huge, heavy metal pallets set against the wall waiting to be lifted, had come down and pinned the man by the chest. His face was swollen and turning black, his eyes bulging.

They heaved off the trays frantically, six or seven men at once, and it needed that many, the trays were solid, but it took time to reach the last, they had fallen on top of one another anyhow.

The machines were still running, they could only see the man, not hear him moaning and then falling silent, in the din.

Tommy was on the end of the last beam as they dragged it off the man.

'George Crab,' someone said, though it had to be read on his lips through the noise.

Another had run across the yard to the offices where there was a telephone, someone else running to the doctor's surgery.

There was blood coming from the man's nose and ears, and his bulging eyes were bloodshot. His arm was bent awkwardly backwards and one leg was twisted over. Someone knelt down and put his head to him to try to tell if his heart was beating.

And then, quite suddenly, as if it were the end of the day, the machines juddered and fell silent and there was only the faint ticking of the metal as it settled and began to cool.

The air seethed with dust. They heard their own breathing.

'He's dead, he's dead,' one of the women shouted. 'It's Ellen Crab's man, someone go for her.'

But the man who had put his head on George Crab's chest looked up, shaking his head.

'His heart's beating all right.'

'Only look at the state of him.'

George Crab moaned, the sound seeming pushed out of his ribcage. The fresh blood trickled out of the corner of his mouth.

'Go for Ellen.'

Tommy Carr was standing at the man's right side, where he had helped to pull off the last metal strut, and as he stood, he felt the heat flood through his body, down from his head and out as if from his heart, and without knowing what he did, he knelt and touched George Crab, first with his right hand then with his left and kept his left hand there on the man's coarse cotton overall.

'Has someone run for Ellen?'

'No, poor woman, leave her, she shouldn't see him in this way, leave her to see him in the hospital.'

'He'll be a dead man by then.'

'His heart was beating, I felt his heart.'

Tommy stayed quite still, the heat coming off him as if he had come out of a fire.

George Crab let out the soft moan again, but then there was the sound of the siren and the urgent voices shouting and the clang of the gates opening.

Tommy got to his feet and almost fell, his legs too weak to bear him. He reached out and clutched one of the wooden pillars and leaned against it.

No one paid him any attention. The footsteps came clattering up the iron stairs. Tommy took a couple of breaths and moved away and then there were the men in blue serge and caps and a stretcher and people saying this, saying that, telling, contradicting.

From the far end of the long room, he watched them carry George Crab away.

Gradually the machines started up and people went silently back to them, gradually things settled to normal, except that no one laughed across a machine at someone else or made a gesture, waved their arms in some joking sign, and when they went for the afternoon breaks, they sat on the iron stairs or the ledge outside the machine room and drank silently, not meeting one another's eyes. They had seen George Crab, seen the blood trickle and the way his chest had looked caved in and even though his heart had been beating they had no thought that he could be alive, or if his heart still managed to pump, then alive for long.

Tommy worked through the afternoon in a daze of exhaustion. People glanced in his direction and away. He was one of them and yet apart, and still a pariah because of what they had heard. They preferred to think about George Crab.

Just as the machines began to shut down at six, word came that he was not dead but terribly injured and that Ellen Crab had been fetched to the hospital. People shook their heads and took off aprons and overalls, lifted jackets and scarves and caps down from the pegs and went home quietly and the air and dust settled in the long room as the door closed.

18

THE WEATHER changed and the sun shone. At midnight, Eve sat on the back step looking at the moonlit garden and the air was still warm, the sky pinpricked all over with bright stars. Bert Ankerby had told her what he knew of the names in the sky – the Bear, the Pleiades, Cassiopeia – and now she tried to pick them out on her own but it was only a pattern and confusion again.

Somewhere on the far side of the field a fox barked.

Tommy was sound asleep in the same way he always slept now, heavy as a stone, never seeming to stir and sometimes scarcely to breathe. He slept like it from the moment he lay down.

The past few weeks had been the strangest he had ever known. He walked off in the morning as usual and for the couple of miles that he was alone he felt free and light of heart, things might almost have been as they used to be. He looked ahead to when he could make out the chimneys and gantries of the works and the smoke and the dust stained the sky, and at once, he changed, he felt anxious and wanted to shrink away, to turn back, to slink close to the walls and fade into them. People saw him. People looked and looked away, or glanced to one another, though plenty peered at him, said this word or that before moving on swiftly.

Strangely, once he went in through the gates of the works he could lose himself among the others and then he felt safe. They worked with him, they had talked themselves dry about him and perhaps there was nothing more to be said. But he knew that the calm could not last and all the time he was working, or sitting out in the sun on the iron staircase or the flat roof during his breaks, he felt uneasily that he would not be left alone like this, that something else would happen to turn his unsteady world upside down again.

George Crab had arrived at the hospital half dead yet with the life reviving in him minute by minute. His wife Ellen had come, her face stained with tears and her eyes full of fear, but when she had seen him sitting up, had said they had no right to try and prepare her for the worst when he was nowhere near death, anyone could see. He was a good colour, he looked himself, apart from a graze on his brow.

'They said you were crushed by the metal racks.'

'I don't recall.'

'They fell on your legs and chest and half crushed you to death, you could barely breathe, you had blood coming from you.'

'I knew I was dying.'

'You cannot have been.'

George shook his head. He spoke the truth when he said he could not recall but he recalled the terrible pain over his heart pressing the breath out of him and the feeling as if a knife were cutting down on his leg. He recalled a man's head bent close to his own, as if he were listening. He had seen blackness and then a terrible redness in front of his eyes and nothing had been clear to him, he could not make out where he was or why.

But then he had felt a few seconds of searing heat, as if they had opened one of the furnaces close to him so that it seemed the whole place was on fire. After that, there had been no pain only a lightness and the desire to sleep and the name of Tommy Carr on his lips.

He had opened his eyes and seen the sky tip from side to side and thought that he was falling forwards but now he realised that he had been carried on a stretcher down the iron staircase.

That was all. He had closed his eyes and slept.

He had tried to sort out words to talk to Ellen about it and the nurse or the doctor, but there did not seem to be words and when a few came out they shushed him, though kindly, so he had fallen silent and let himself drift back to sleep. When he woke next the blinds had been drawn down against the windows and he had a terrible thirst. They brought him a pitcher of water and he drank it all but did not try to say anything else.

They had wanted to keep him in the hospital but he was having none of it, he was fit. He got out of the bed and walked up and down to prove it to them, so that they let him go, striding out through the doors into the street with Ellen a step behind.

Word was fire and raced round town as it had done before and no one knew what to make of any of it, or what to do or say, and so George Crab was feted and clapped on the back and Tommy Carr was left alone, for you never knew.

It had taken Tommy a long time to walk home one night and when Eve saw him from the window her heart turned because he looked as he had looked before, his shoulders bent, his head down. But he came into the house with a light enough step and she saw that he was not as he had been, he was stronger, and although he would never be a stout man he had lost the terrible thinness, his belt was fastened a few notches looser.

But she asked 'Tommy?' as he sat down, for there was surely something. Something.

He shook his head.

'Has something happened? Has something been said? Are you not well?'

'I'm fine, Eve.'

'No.'

But he would not say more, only asked about one or two things to do with the garden and the new rabbits and the way of the world and she knew she should wait. Tommy did things and said things in his own time or not at all.

He walked to the bottom of the garden and looked over the fields and walked back, stopping to look at this or that, but she saw that he was struggling to make sense of things from the way he frowned and seemed to be absent from himself.

And then he did tell her, as she went about gathering the last scraps for the chickens.

'Would the man have died?'

He shook his head. 'Who knows the answer to that? Not me. I know nothing.'

'And you've done nothing.'

'Have I not?'

'Nothing wrong, surely to God.'

'I don't know what has happened or will but I'm treated like a man with a running sore, that I do know.'

But in this he was wrong. He was not being shunned. People were puzzled and they were also respectful of him, not wanting to intrude, seeing the troubled look on him and thinking they would help by leaving him alone.

Only talk went on, talk and speculation and wonderment, and questioning and what had been vague and uncertain firmed as it was talked about and seemed to become clearer and better known. Mary Ankerby had had a stroke or a seizure and come round as if it were nothing more than a moment of dizziness. George Crab had been crushed almost to death and pinned to the ground by the weight of the metal racks, so that blood had been squeezed from his mouth and his eyes had bulged, and that night had walked out of the hospital and home, as well as anyone in the town.

And all of it, including his own recovery, had to do with Tommy Carr.

On hearing the tale from another woman in the street, Miriam laughed, her usual short, scornful laugh, and would hear none of it, for the town was always swirling with talk of something.

The weekend after the accident to George Crab was as hot as it had been that year and Eve had got up just after first light because she could not sleep and she liked to be outside in the cool pearly dawn before the day staled. It was a morning when the presence of Jeannie was again as strong as strong, the child pottering after her, catching hold of her skirt and clapping her hands as the chickens came fluttering and flapping out of their house. Eve did not cry for her daughter now, but when it happened in this way a shadow of sadness fell over the day and she could not enjoy the sight or smell or taste of things. She thought she would walk across the fields and up to the churchyard later, in the cooler evening, and as she was thinking it, became aware that someone was coming along the path, she supposed a visitor to one of the other cottages.

But the woman continued past them to the gate of number 6. Eve did not know her but she saw women like her every time she went into the town, older than their years, grey before their time, a bad colour and with front teeth missing and twisted feet in shoes that were made to fit someone else.

'Hello?'

Eve looked up.

'I don't want to trouble you. It's Tommy I have to see, Tommy Carr.'

Eve was sure she had never seen the woman before and when she said her name, Doreen Willis, it meant nothing.

'My husband's in the house.'

Abruptly, the woman burst into tears.

Sitting in the kitchen, her hands shaking, clutching the mug of tea Eve had made, Doreen Willis took a long time to compose herself and Eve could only look on and wait until she heard Tommy's footsteps on the stairs. The woman looked up, her face fearful. She had said nothing except that she must see Tommy but when he came into the small kitchen she got up in panic and backed away.

'Mrs Willis,' Eve said. 'It's you she has come for.'

She went to pour his tea. The mistiness of early morning had dissolved away and the sky was clear, the sun already bright.

Nothing was said by any of them. Tommy stood looking uncertain, Doreen Willis was standing as if frozen to the ground.

Then he said gently, 'What is it I can do for you?'

She let out a small breath. 'Leonard,' she said. 'You know my son. Leonard?'

'Leonard Willis the apprentice, yes. I'm sorry, I should have known at once. But I haven't seen him about the works for some while.'

'He can't. His lungs are full up with it. He can hardly catch any breath.'

Tuberculosis then, Eve knew at once, for it was rampant in the town where the air was thick and fetid with smoke and fumes and dust from the chimneys, and the germs bred in the small houses crowded with too many people. She had sometimes wondered how Miriam's children survived it, but they always seemed fit as fleas no matter what the state of the house or the lack of decent food.

'Will you come?'

Tommy looked embarrassed. He had not told Eve, feeling oddly ashamed, but it was not the first time he had been asked in the last weeks to go to someone who was sick, grown men, women, children, babies. Word had travelled. He was talked about. Suddenly, people needed him.

He had always refused, telling them they must see the doctor or the district nurse, go to the hospital, go to priest or parson even, for he could do nothing, why would they think it, and he had no right to try.

Doreen's face had fallen in on itself with a desperate sadness. She sat down heavily at the table again.

'You should see the doctor,' Tommy said.

'The doctor can't help. He's a good man but he can't help. Fresh air, he said, sea air or the mountains. That's what cures people but how can we give him those things?' She looked straight into Tommy's face. 'You can help.'

Eve had taken no part, not believing it had to do with her, but now she said only, 'You should go, Tommy.'

'I have no right.'

'If it does no good you won't be to blame but if you don't go at all won't you blame yourself?'

After a long moment of silence, he nodded.

19

And so it began, for he went to see the Willis boy, whose skin was damp and who coughed almost without ceasing, and sat with him, touching his forehead once. A look of astonishment came over Leonard's face and he jerked away from Tommy's hand as if it had burned him.

When Tommy had left the house the boy had fallen asleep. He slept for fourteen hours and awoke with his pallor gone and his skin cool and dry.

After that, there was someone at the gates of the works or at the door of 6 The Cottages every day, and sometimes two or three people, wanting him to go to someone sick, someone in pain, an old man dying, a woman with a tumour, a child with a fever, people racked with coughs and people bleeding, and Tommy went to as many as he could manage.

Almost every time, the heat passed through him to the sick man or woman or child, though not every time were they well afterwards, for some died, but they died well, their breathing easy, their pain faded to nothing, and died as if that was what they had meant and longed to do.

Eve grew used to strangers coming to the door and having to tell them that he was not home. Some of them simply waited by the gate, others went away, to return in the evening. They troubled her. Once a woman brought a limp and sickly infant who lay inert in her arms and Eve was terrified the child would die.

At the gates of the works, people were turned away, and inside, Tommy was left alone to his work but sometimes given strange glances. When the looks were hostile, he was hurt and wanted to stop the machines and, while the long room was quiet, try to find words to tell them that he was the same man, the same friend, and beg them to treat him as they used to. But how could they?

The town buzzed with story after story, often exaggerated and embroidered, for sometimes a sickness was little enough or only fleeting and nothing Tommy's presence did affected it. People were well again as they would have been in any case.

He tried to hide himself among the mass of the others coming out of the works after the hooters sounded at the end of the day, but they moved away from him, revealing his presence to anyone who was waiting to ask him to come here, go there. He wanted only to dodge down a side street to the canal towpath and so out onto the country road, walking steadily alone and relishing the clearer air and the quietness as he got nearer and nearer to The Cottages. He was tired. The work was hard and relentless, his ears hummed with the constant noise and sometimes his head ached. In this he was the same as they all were, battered into exhaustion by the din. He longed to feel his hand on the gate and his feet on the grassy path and to see Eve in the window or among the plants or at the chicken house. And always he remembered Jeannie Eliza there with her.

People who needed him were not the only ones who came to the house. The newspapers were sent to talk to him, and when he would not see them, tried to get words out of Eve's mouth. She would not speak for Tommy or say anything for herself, and so in frustration the papers printed lies and told tales and the word spread further and letters began to come. People read about Tommy and asked him to travel to them. The letters lay opened on the table and Tommy looked at them, read them again, turned them face down or put them back into their envelopes in despair.

'I can't,' he said.

Eve touched the back of his head gently. 'No. People have no right to expect it.'

But he was eaten up with guilt that he refused anyone.

The heat broke with two nights of tremendous thunderstorms and rain that washed the stones down from the peak and filled the ditches to overflowing. The sky was livid night and morning and Eve was afraid that the lightning would rip down through it to strike the chicken house or their own chimney.

In the morning the air was warm and soupy with moisture and the sky hung low over the houses. Tommy had been more tired than usual and got himself ready slowly and did not want to leave.

At the works, the gatekeeper handed him an envelope. He stood to one side, turning it over anxiously. Someone else wanted him to go to them, someone he would agonise over and long to avoid but see out of guilt, though why he should feel guilt he did not understand.

But the envelope did not contain any letter begging him to visit someone sick. It held only his dismissal.

* * *

138

Tommy understood. There had been talk since the beginning, his presence distracted some and then there were the people at the gate waiting to see him and even those inside the works wanting his advice, though he had none to give. He had nothing to collect, no reason to go in, he simply signed the paper that was put in front of him and turned away. A few stragglers running in late glanced at him but most did not, they were preoccupied with their own hurry. Before he had walked far, the streets had emptied of any who had work to go to and were being taken over by the workless and the women gossiping at doors and the children. He was dazed and walked slowly, a stranger at this hour in the town, feeling the sidelong looks and hearing the murmurs.

The canal was gleaming under the sun, the grass dry and rubbed away with the absence of rain and the trample of feet. Boys fished. A barge slid past. Tommy sat on an old beam that served for a bench and looked into the water, not knowing. Not knowing. He knew that he had been dying. His stomach had been like a bag full of red-hot coals and his chest had hurt him when he breathed, he had barely been able to turn his head. He had wanted to die in order to escape through a door which would lead to the absence of pain and because there was nothing left in his life to hold to, even Eve. And then those few moments of burning heat through his body had changed every-thing and he was well, fitter and stronger and more full of energy and life than he thought he had ever been.

But then? He did not know. Why could it not have stopped there? Being able to restore health and even life back to other people, which is what he seemed to do now, should have been a gift and a blessing. Instead, it had led to his being here, idling by the canal, workless and ashamed.

He had no need to feel shame. He knew it. He was not responsible for any of it, not guilty of anything, but knowledge and reason had no power over him when set against the shame.

He had been proud of his trade which he had done since he had been a boy apprentice and he was skilled for nothing else even if there had been any other work in the town. Now he was one of the many hollow-eyed men with worn-out clothes and shoes and dirty caps, hanging about the streets, gathering by the war memorial, saying little, passing a single roll-up round among themselves.

He got up and went along the towpath. A white dog with a black ear stopped to sniff at him and crouched to be patted. When he walked on, it followed him a little way before disappearing fast up a ginnel after a thin cat. He had wanted a dog. When Jeannie Eliza had been older, they said, then it would be right to get one, company for her and to get her properly used to animals other than the rabbits and chickens, for those were not pets and she would have to learn it.

Every so often Tommy felt a moment of strangeness and wondered briefly what he was doing out here in the sunshine and the quiet, watching the boys fish and the barge slide by, before he remembered. He could not take in that he was not going back to the works. He had never known anything else.

He would have to go home soon, tell Eve, see the fear on her face, that they had become what they had never thought to become, one of the households with a jobless man, struggling, making do, and having no hope that it would change. They were better off than many, if having no family meant being better off, and they lived simply, bought little, had one another for company. They would manage and Eve would never reproach him for his dismissal, no matter what the reason – and no reason had been given to him. But he did not need one. He knew. They all knew.

Yet still he felt ashamed.

20

WORD SPREAD again and again, brought people to number 6 The Cottages. After a week it brought a letter, from someone living in a village on the other side of the peak, to which word had also travelled.

My daughter, who is twenty years old, has been crippled for eleven years after falling from her horse. She is not paralysed but able to move only with great difficulty, and is in extreme and constant pain. Doctors can do nothing more for her. She is in despair and threatens to take her own life.

We have heard of you and I am asking if you will come to Daphne and try, if not to cure her, at least to give her relief from her pain.

I will naturally pay whatever sum of money you require.

Tommy's first reaction was of anger, which startled Eve for he was rarely out of temper. He had taken his dismissal sombrely but with the patience and acceptance she would have expected. She was the one who had been angry then, not with him but with those who now mistrusted him, were suspicious and wanted no part of him.

'I am not for hire,' he said after reading the letter.

'But if this is the way you have of earning your bread, what is wrong with that? You would be out of pocket if you had to travel there.'

'I am not for hire. Whatever has happened, it is not something I can take money for. How do I know if any of it has to do with me?'

'But you do know.'

'No,' he said quietly. 'I know what happened to me but all the rest . . . It is likely to be chance. I am claiming nothing, I understand none of it. And I am not for hire.'

'Then go to see her without being hired.'

He was silent but after a day wrote that he was not able to help, though he felt badly about it as he walked to post his letter.

'I would be afraid,' he said. 'I can't set myself up in that way. It would be wrong.'

'Why would it?'

But he simply shook his head.

He had been right that they were better off than most although he was without work, but that did not make things easy, and Eve fretted that they might have to leave 6 The Cottages at the end of the year if they could not find money enough for the rent.

Tommy walked all over the district looking for work for he could turn his hand to many things in the house and garden and even on the land and surely someone would need a labourer. But there were too many seeking and too few hiring and each time he returned without an employment apart from once, when he got work with a gang of men ditching, for a few days.

He saw that Eve's face was set in lines of tiredness and worry and that she smiled little and kept glancing at him as if about to say something before changing her mind. She went to see Miriam and stayed for over a week to help with the children, set the house to rights, mended trousers and shirts and jackets and cooked proper food, saw that they were all clean, though she knew that once she had left things would revert to their old state. The boys were growing and rarely ill, which was a miracle. They fought and

144

tumbled about and spent the days of that summer fishing the canal and roaring round the streets with gangs of others.

Miriam sat in the chair on the back step watching without interest while Eve nursed the baby, a scrawny, sickly boy whose skin was tinged yellow from early jaundice.

'Doctors are rich men,' Miriam said.

'Are they? They work hard for their money then.'

'And look how many still die.'

'We all die, don't we? They can't hold it off for ever, even if they are doctors.'

'Tommy could be a rich man, couldn't he? He's done as well as any of them. He's a fool, sitting idle when he could use the gift he's been given.'

Eve rocked the baby and, after a moment, had to get up to tend Arthur George who came in from the street howling with a grazed knee, but as she did so, she could not dismiss from her mind what Miriam had said.

She had long given up trying to suggest to her sister that there should be no more children, though sometimes she made a sharp remark to John Bullard, who chose not to hear. But when she left to return home she worried about the boys, who might not be unhappy or ill but who did not get enough good food to eat and about whom nobody seemed to take any trouble. True, they helped one another and grew up somehow unscathed, but what had they to hope for?

'The man, Mr Arnold, wrote again,' Tommy said the evening she got home. 'It seems as if his daughter will try to do away with herself if she suffers more.'

She knew what he was saying.

'You would walk to Hoargate and then catch a bus?'

'Yes.'

'Well.'

She took the spade from beside the door and went to dig up potatoes. Bert Ankerby had two marrows for her which he was in the act of bringing and so they went down the garden together, talking of what she might grow for the winter for he was anxious to make sure they had as much as might be possible, anxious that if Tommy did not get work soon they should still manage. That they lived mainly on eggs and potatoes and whatever vegetables they grew bothered neither of them. The rabbits had gone for the pot and provided suppers for a week.

The next morning Tommy got up at five and was at Hoargate waiting for the bus by six. He should be there by nine, though how long a walk he would have after the bus let him off he did not know.

In fact the stop was not far from the gate of the house, which was called 'Laverings', and he was walking up the drive before eight thirty. He had not let them know he was coming, thinking that the girl would not have gone anywhere and that as they had asked for him he would not be turned away.

He was not, but seeing the house, a large stone one with pillars at the entrance, long windows onto a lawn, a gravel drive round to stables, he almost turned round. He was not a man who ever felt troubled about his origins, he felt able to speak to anyone, hold his head up anywhere, and had always been respected for it. But walking up to this door he felt like a pedlar.

There was no need. He asked for Mr Arnold and gave his name and within a few seconds the man came into the hall and took hold of both his hands, holding them warmly and stumbling over words of thanks.

Tommy was offered breakfast but accepted only a cup of strong tea which he drank standing, hardly liking to glance round. But what he saw was not stately or imposing, it was solid and comfortable, everything good, everything well made, but still part of a proper home. Mr Arnold was a tall, broad man with a thick head of hair and a high forehead, a good suit, a watch chain. An honest look.

'There is no one else,' he said as they made for the

staircase after Tommy had drunk his tea quickly and hot. 'I had no one else to turn to. Daphne is little alone, though we try not to let her feel she is being watched, but when she spoke of taking her life . . .' They went along a wide corridor with a window at the far end overlooking parkland. The sun was climbing up the sky now. It would be hot.

'You were the only person I could think of turning to. Everyone speaks of you. You have done wonderful things.'

'I don't know what I do,' Tommy said. 'I came because I felt for you but I may have nothing to give. I may be of no help. I can make you no promises.'

He felt nervous and as if he were some sort of impostor, for he had no confidence, no sense of sureness about what the outcome of it all might be. He felt a hollowness in the pit of his stomach. He had no right to have come and would have gone back down the quiet corridor and away if they had not stopped at a white-painted door on which Mr Arnold tapped, before beckoning Tommy to follow him.

She was sitting in a deep armchair beside the windows. Her hair was dark and tied back from her face, which was a pleasing face and would have been young and might have been pretty, if it had not been marked by years of illness and pain and of sitting alone looking out of a window. A book was on the arm of the chair but it was not open.

'This is Mr Carr,' her father said. 'I told you about him.'

She looked round and directly at Tommy. 'He was not going to come.'

'We thought not but he has.'

'Why did you change your mind?'

Tommy hesitated. 'I thought I should. I couldn't rest.'

'What happens now?'

For a second he almost said that he did not know, that he had not been taught, that he was as unsure of it all as anyone, but then it came to him that he did know, and this was nothing new or strange. Miss Arnold was no different.

He went across the room where an upright chair stood against the wall, and lifted it and set it down beside her.

'Do you need anything?'

'No.'

'Do you chant and say prayers?'

'No.'

Mr Arnold was still standing.

'Give me your hand please.'

She stretched it out to him and he took it. It was small and soft and cool to his touch.

For a few moments they sat in silence until he felt a flutter of doubt, wondered if he would fail and why and what he might say to them.

Her eyes were on his face and he saw despair in them. And then he felt the heat rush up through his body until his skin and flesh and even the blood in his veins burned, and as he felt it so he saw that she did, it transferred itself from him until he began to feel drained and tired. He took his hand away from hers and sat for a moment. The young woman had closed her eyes and her pale skin was slightly flushed.

There was a great silence in the room.

21

Mr Arnold offered him fifty pounds, which he refused, and then, assuming it was because fifty pounds was too little, Mr Arnold suggested one hundred, but Tommy would take no money except for his fare.

Two days later, a letter arrived. Daphne Arnold had been in no pain since his visit and was now able to walk about the garden, though it would take time for her muscles to strengthen fully. The envelope contained a cheque which Tommy tore up at once before going out to pick the last beans and take down their sticks.

Eve did not know what she felt. She was proud of him for refusing the payment, to which he said he had no right, but money was so short now and there seemed no chance of anyone employing him in the town, even if there had been work.

And every day someone came to the door, someone sick or with a sick child or husband or wife, wanting him to go back with them or sometimes to see them there and then. He always did.

Word travelled further, people came from many miles away, letters arrived asking him to travel here and there about the country.

'Miracle worker?'

'The Healer.'

'Is this man a saint or a fraud?'

Those things were written in the newspapers and more besides and when he went into the town, he was shunned or embraced and did not know how to deal with either. He felt awkward and sometimes ashamed and would say, 'I do nothing.' Or, 'I don't know what happens.' But most often he remained silent.

One day, as he was coming out of the grocer's shop with the few things they could not manage without buying, he saw Dr McElvey.

'Tommy.'

He stopped.

'I have been hoping to see you.'

'Doctor.'

'Will you come to the surgery? There is something I must say.'

'Say it here.'

'No, it will not do for the open street. I have a patient to see. I will meet you there.'

He had looked at Tommy out of cold eyes and they were cold when he greeted him without a word at the door of the surgery. The room was empty but somehow the air seethed with all the sickness and pain and fear that crammed it full for hours of the day.

They went into the consulting room.

'You know why I asked you here.'

Tommy stood, as he had not been asked to sit, and did not answer.

'You know what happened to you, Tommy?'

Tommy shook his head for he did not but the doctor was not waiting for his answer.

'I will tell you. My diagnosis was incorrect. That is perfectly possible, I am only a humble physician. I believed you to have malignant tumours but clearly you did not. Whatever the swellings were that caused your pain and weakness must have been benign – some form of cysts. Those can disappear as they appeared and why we do not know. Once they had disappeared you recovered speedily, as would be expected. And that is all, Tommy.'

Tommy was so shocked that his throat seemed to close up and he could not speak. Thoughts swirled round his head but he stood dumb.

'And now all this wildfire talk round the town of healings and cures . . . this is nonsense, and you know it. It goes against medical science and it goes against common sense. You are not a doctor.'

'I know that,' he said loudly and it was easy to speak it out. 'I know that well and I have never pretended to it.'

'Perhaps not, but you have gone along with what the people have said and never denied the rumours, you have visited sick people pretending to be able to cure them, you have –'

'I have done none of that. None of it. I have gone with people when they begged me, but not easily, not without great doubts.'

'Mary Ankerby.'

'Mary is my neighbour.'

'It is said you cured her after she suffered some form of stroke or seizure and was near to death.'

'I cannot help what people say. I have not said it.'

'People come to your door and you take them in and attempt to cure them of all manner of sicknesses. You go to houses in the town where desperate people will believe anything and resort to anything in their distress.'

'No.'

'And now you are casting your net wider and taking payment. You are a deceiver and a beguiler, you are obtaining money from the weak and the poor and the sick, you are –'

'NO.' Tommy heard his own voice raised in angry denial. He did not shout. He was never angry. This was not as he knew himself to be, but what the doctor was saying was so untrue and so wrong that he could not have spoken in any other way.

'Deny these things.'

'I do deny them.'

'I can call any number of witnesses. I am the doctor in this town. People speak to me. People ask me questions. People tell me things.'

'I have done no wrong and made no claims. I only know what I do know.'

'And what do you know, Tommy Carr?'

He knew that he had been dying, that the pain he had suffered over so many weeks, and the weakness and the sickness, the way he had been unable to eat and scarcely to keep down water and become as thin as one of his own bean sticks, all of those things had been real and his disease had been malignant and incurable. He knew it and knew that Dr McElvey had known it. He knew.

And he knew that he had felt a great heat course through his body and afterwards he had been well. He knew that whatever sickness had been with those people who were touched by him and by his heat had immediately left them and they were well. He knew that he did not know how or why, but that he knew and they knew, he could not doubt.

That was all he knew.

Yet as he stood there, with the doctor's cold eyes and hard voice confronting him, he also knew that he could not defend himself and nor could the people who had come to him defend him. If they were asked, perhaps they would speak for him, or perhaps they would not but instead would retreat out of fear and shame and because they were anxious not to upset the ordered way of things or to anger the doctor who had always served them without sparing himself or taking from them a penny more than he needed.

Tommy said, 'I have taken no money and I have not asked for anyone to come to me. You will believe me or you will not and I cannot blame you for minding what you think I have done. You are the only person who has the right to do so. But I am saddened that you want to deny what we both know, not about anyone else, I cannot speak for them, but about me. You know how it was with me, as well as I know. I was to have died, perhaps that day or that night after you saw me. You know what you know as well as I and yet you deny it now and that is wrong and it grieves me. Why you do it I can't know. It surely doesn't reflect on you. You were goodness itself to me, as you are to others. I don't understand you but I could never pretend to you and I do not lie to you. And you know that.'

After he had left, Dr McElvey stood at the window for a long time, angry at first that Tommy Carr had defied him but gradually, as he calmed, struggling to admit to himself that he had spoken no more than the truth. He had been dying. His tumours would have overwhelmed his system and there had been little left in him with which to fight. Why had he pretended otherwise?

But as to the rest of it, that enraged him – the rumours and stories and fantasies the town was seething with, the tales in the papers. Tommy could not help what was said, but he added fuel to the flames by agreeing to see those who were sick and without any other hope and who turned to him in error.

He should refuse. He was wrong and he ought to pay for that wrong, or suffer for it.

Dr McElvey was a proud man and knew his own worth. He had liked Tommy Carr and felt great sorrow for him in the death of his child and in his own terrible sickness, but he could not tolerate a man such as he was taking the sick people of the town to himself.

His anger curdled his temper for the rest of the day and those who came to his surgery afterwards felt the brunt of it. But late that night, walking out into the humid, close air before he slept, he had to accept that there was almost certainly nothing he could do other than warn Tommy Carr again and make it known about the place how much he himself was angered by it all.

In the middle of the night he woke. The air had not cooled and even with the windows wide open the closeness was oppressive. He lay still for a long time wondering what it was that had cured Tommy Carr and why. The questioning kept him awake until long after the breaking of a sultry dawn.

22

THE HENS stopped laying and there had been no train for weeks, so that the ground yielded less and less.

Eve went looking for work and found it, for the mornings from five to eight o'clock, swabbing floors and cleaning down machines in one of the works. It was hard and her arms and back ached so that at first she could barely walk home upright, but after a time she was used to it and stronger. The money was poor but it meant the worry was less, though Tommy felt shame that he could not find work himself and walked into the town twice a week asking at the different factories. He found nothing. At the printworks the gatekeeper told him there was no point in asking, men were now being laid off even there. The chair factory had shut down.

The town looked shabbier and more grey-spirited, the people down at heel and sad-eyed, though the children played as cheerfully as ever and boys still fished in the canal and roared about the streets on makeshift carts and kicked old shoes tied up with string.

The granite-grey church gave out soup and bread every day at noon and the queue began to form an hour before, the children hanging round for biscuits and extra crusts and racing away again when their fists closed over them. Tommy would not go and in any case they still had enough. When the hens laid, Eve brought eggs in, some to sell to the shop, a few to give away to the women she worked with.

The doctor did not come near them again and people still sent for Tommy and came to the house and Tommy still saw them, though never out of pride or defiance.

A few weeks after Eve had begun working, he received another letter from Mr Arnold, asking him to visit.

My elderly mother has recently come to live with us and is patience itself but is in great pain with arthritis, especially in her hands which she finds useless for any purpose as a result. If you would come to see her and could do even a little of what you did for Daphne, we would be in your debt.

'He should be paid,' Miriam said, spreading dabs of dripping onto toast. The eggs Eve had brought were for the two of them. John Bullard still slept, as he did most days until ten or eleven in the morning. After that he went to the men's club.

'You working until your fingers are raw and him doing sweet nothing.'

Eve looked at her in amazement but Miriam did not see the irony of what she had said.

'Tommy does more good than most, why shouldn't he be paid?'

'He doesn't see it in that way.'

'You can.'

'He wouldn't live with himself.'

Miriam shouted for the boys. The youngest clung to Eve's legs trying to haul himself up. She lifted him though her back ached badly, as ever after the morning's work.

The boys poured in and grabbed their food, piled out again noisily. School began the next week which gave the older ones a hot dinner. It made a difference. Any small thing that did so was welcomed.

The kitchen went quiet. The baby slept, the toddler sat under the table chewing his bread, the other young ones on the step eating and playing with a small heap of stones. If she could always have felt at ease like this in her sister's company Eve would have come often, but the peaceful times were rare. Miriam was usually angry or resentful, bitter or full of complaint, and she was not to blame for it though she had made her own choice. But how do we know how our choices will turn out for us? Eve thought. The luck falls one way or it falls the other.

'You could take him,' Miriam said, as Arthur George came in for more bread. 'He's the best of them. He's kind and loving and quieter than the others.'

Eve did not realise what her sister was saying. 'Take him where?'

'Home. It'd fill the space she left you.'

'You think Jeannie Eliza just left a space to be filled? You'd send one of yours away without a thought?'

'I have thought.'

Arthur George had gone out to the others and the heap of stones.

Miriam's face was set hard.

'He's yours. You're his mother and he has his brothers. He has his father.'

Miriam laughed.

'You'd give him away like that?'

'You're my sister. You're family. It's not like giving away.'

Eve got up and because she could not trust herself to speak, because she might have burst into tears of rage and bewilderment at what her sister had said as if it were nothing of consequence, she went out and was half way home before she knew it.

But when she got there, and found Tommy gone and the letter from Mr Arnold on the table, and the kitchen bright with sunlight, then she cried, for Miriam's unloved brood of boys and for the death of her own child, and for the empty house. If she had not known quite surely that it would be wrong, she would have gone straight back and fetched Arthur George and had him for company and, she realised suddenly, to fill the silent space that indeed Jeannie Eliza had left.

The air was heavy with sulphurous clouds gathering like a boil over the peak. She sat on the step as Miriam's boys had done, and finding a few stones around her feet made them into a small pile and moved them into lines and rings and squares. Before long she would have to scrat around in the dry soil for any last potatoes, though she had done so already for days and found none. The carrots were shrivelled and full of holes, the marrows small and hollow. Rain would come now but it was too late to save anything.

Bert Ankerby came down his own path whistling.

No man was more cheerful, day in, day out and no matter what.

She scooped the stones up in the hollow of her hand and tipped them out again to see how they would fall, did so again, and then again. Thunder rumbled in the distance and the sky darkened.

23

THE STORM broke as he walked from the bus, so that he arrived at the door with his clothes soaking wet and his boots, which he had tried to patch and mend himself, letting in the rain.

It was not Mr Arnold who opened the door but a servant, who looked at Tommy with disdain before leading him to a back room to take off his wet things. He handed him an old gardening jacket and a pair of rubber boots. Tommy felt embarrassed under the man's scrutiny, ashamed when his clothes were taken away to be dried while he was led back into the hall.

It was empty. The man disappeared on silent feet. He heard the murmur of voices from a room nearby. The sky beyond the two long windows was blue-black and once or twice lightning zigzagged down it and with the thunder seemed about to crack it open, like a fissure running down a rock.

And then Mr Arnold came across the hall.

'Will you come through? My daughter is away but I know she would wish me to give you her greeting. She is quite well, quite well. We cannot thank you enough.'

'You need not.'

Mr Arnold lowered his voice. 'You did not cash my cheque. It troubles me that you have gone without any reward.'

'I want none.'

He was anxious to dismiss the subject, as always feeling fraudulent when he was thanked or people tried to pay him in whatever way.

They went into a small bright sitting room with windows onto the side lawn.

'My mother.' Arnold gestured to an old woman, small and frail as a bird, who watched the storm from a straight-backed chair. She had a puff of fine white hair like the head of a dandelion, the pink of her scalp showing beneath it.

'Mr Carr?'

Tommy nodded. He felt a stranger to himself, standing in this elegant room wearing a garden jacket and boots that were not his own.

'Are you in pain?'

Her eyes were bright, her skin papery pale as the discs of honesty.

She nodded and put out her hands to him. The joints were swollen, shining and horribly bent.

'I can only give you what I give to everyone. I don't know how or what it is but it seems to be of help to people. I will hold my hands out to you and you take the heat from them into yourself. Nothing else.'

She nodded.

He reached out and took her hands and held them lightly in his own.

The storm was drifting away, the room was lighter, with rain on the windows.

People asked him if he prayed but he did not and he thought of nothing, he merely touched and felt the heat flow from him. Nothing else. Nothing more.

Tommy held the small hands in his own and after a moment the heat rose through him until he was burning. He saw Mrs Arnold's eyes widen with surprise and she stared down at their hands as if she might see fire.

The heat faded, seeming to thin out like a cloud dispersing.

'It has gone,' she said quietly. 'The pain has quite gone.'

'You should rest now. It is tiring and you will sleep, perhaps for some time.' He stood.

'Yes.'

The room was still and quiet. Then Arnold said, 'I must offer you some refreshment. What will you take?'

'A glass of cold water. Thank you.'

Mrs Arnold was leaning back, her eyes closed, her face changed, as if someone had brushed away years and left her as she had been before the illness.

'You should help her upstairs soon,' Tommy said to Mr Arnold. 'She will want to sleep comfortably.'

'Indeed, but first, please come into my study and have your refreshment, if water is all you really want.'

'It is.'

A carafe of it, with a glass, was brought in by the man who had provided Tommy with the jacket and boots, and he drank it down.

It was always the same, this immense thirst. While he did so, Mr Arnold sat at his desk.

'These are hard times,' he said, 'and there is no employment or likely to be. I insist on giving you some payment.'

'No. Thank you. I will take my fare, no more.'

The man shook his head. 'Come, man, what use is pride these days? Pride will not feed and clothe you and keep the roof over your head.'

'I cannot take payment. I know it would be wrong.'

'How do you know?'

Tommy did not answer.

'Why?'

But he did not know that either.

He turned away.

The sky through the hall windows was pearl pale, the storm over. It was not the supercilious man but Mr Arnold who came with Tommy's own jacket and boots, warm from the drying.

Eve was in when he got home. She looked up at him and he saw pain in her face.

'It was reaching up,' she said, 'my back twisted. They said not to go in again.'

'Until it's rested?'

'Not to go back. They can't have people who aren't up to the work.'

He put his hand on her arm and she leaned against him. But her eyes were dry. She did not feel pity for herself.

'I'll see if there's any work maybe sitting down at one of the benches.'

But they both knew there would not be.

There came the click of the gate and steps on the path and when Tommy went out he found a man and a child.

'Would you see the boy? He has a terrible rash of boils.'

And so the day went on and by dark he had seen four others and every day there would be more. When he slept he was so heavy and still for hour after hour Eve wondered if he breathed.

Late that night, when the last of them had gone and she was already in bed, he picked his jacket off the chair back and felt something deep in the pocket that he had not noticed, and reaching in, found an envelope. Inside the envelope were four folded notes for fifty pounds each. He had never held so much money in his hand. He got up and went to open the door and the smell of the garden after rain was sweet but it did not lift his heart as it should.

He was happy that Eve was no longer getting up at dawn to do work which had made her ill and in any case paid so little, but he could not get work himself.

The sky had cleared. It was cool. The year was drifting down.

Why was he so sure that he should not keep Mr Arnold's money? It had been freely given and for a second time.

He went back and looked at the notes. Touched them.

Then he folded them back carefully into his pocket, locked the door and went upstairs. Eve woke as he went into the room and he could see that the bedclothes were disarranged where she had been turning and lying different ways to try and ease the pain in her back.

'You look troubled, Tom.'

'No, no.' He set his jacket on the back of the chair. 'Things will get better. Everyone says.'

'They will.'

She sighed and turned over again. Sometimes he was in the room, sitting or lying next to her, but not there at all, she could not reach him through the stone wall of his own thoughts and so it was now. She knew better than to pester him. If he had something to say to her he would say it.

But it seemed that he had nothing.

It had begun to rain again and Eve lay listening to it patter on the window and wished that things would change in some way, though most of all, change back, so that Tommy had his work and she had Jeannie Eliza and none of the rest of it had ever come about.

24

Tommy thought about it for two full days and on the third decided that he would keep Mr Arnold's money. He put three of the banknotes into his clothes drawer and took one into the town where he exchanged it for others, some worth five and the rest one-pound and ten-shilling notes. Into an envelope he counted enough to pay their rent for a whole year and walked with it to the office of the landlord, getting a receipt in return, after which he felt as if he had been relieved of a great burden. Eve loved the cottage and he knew that having to leave would break her. If he had worried about anything it had been that and he had accepted Mr Arnold's money to be sure that they could remain there.

But he spent a little more of it on a cornflower-blue

scarf for Eve, and, as an afterthought, a bar of rose-scented soap wrapped in paper. Carrying his purchases home, he remembered the day he had met her, when she had dropped her brown-paper parcel into the canal and he had rescued it for her. As he had grown up he had watched the young men around him find girls and make them wives and start families and had naturally felt that he would do so too but not understood how to choose. He had looked at some and they were pretty, at others and they were pert, at the ones with kind faces and the hard ones, the laughing ones, the sad and those old before they had had time to be young, but walking by the canal he had seen Eve and she was different. How she was and why and what made him know it, he had wondered every day since.

When he walked in, she was lying on the stone floor of the kitchen trying to ease her back. Tommy knelt down and saw the creases of pain on her face and the clouding of it in her eyes.

'Shall I help you up to bed now?'

'I'm better here, the mattress on the bed bends my back.'

'I brought you this,' he said, reaching in his pocket for the soap with its rose scent that had made his jacket smell of the flower. 'I should have thought before – you don't have enough of pretty things, nice things to enjoy.

'It's been wrong of me to help others and not you.'

Eve looked at him anxiously.

'Take my hands.'

She did so and he saw how much the movement hurt her.

Her hands were no longer the hands of a young woman, although that surely was what she was still, they had been worn thin and roughened by work.

'The money was freely given,' he said quickly. 'I didn't *ask* for payment and never would. You know it.'

'It's what you think is best. It's not for me to say.'

'This is best.'

'I know you are a good man.'

'No. I do what I have been given to do, nothing else.'

He had been holding her hands for several minutes, waiting for the heat to come and flow through him to Eve.

It did not come.

Ten minutes went by and it did not come.

'You can't help me,' Eve said, 'because I am not a stranger to you.'

'Why do you think that?'

'It just feels as if it would.'

'No. But I think you should get up, the stone is so cold.'

She sat on a hard chair by the kitchen table, and again, Tommy took her hands and then touched her shoulders, her head, her arm, and at last, held his own hands against her back.

But the heat did not come.

Later, after Eve had gone to bed and he had tried to make her comfortable, he went out into the quiet autumn night and began to walk, knowing the track by heart and not needing the half-moon's light to guide him. There would be frosts soon – the faint smell of winter had been on the air these past days, but not now. He walked steadily along the track under the wide dark sky and the wire that had tightened and tightened in his body gradually slackened until he felt easy again. He took the track round the side of the peak and made for the road towards the wood. A fox's eyes gleamed briefly out of the darkness, something scuttled across his path and into the undergrowth. He walked on, for many miles and several hours, before turning for home, and in all that way and for all that time he neither saw nor heard another human soul.

25

SLOWLY, EVE's pain lessened and her back grew stronger. She was able to walk down the garden and to prepare their food, though Tommy did the heavy work and anything that meant she would have had to lift or bend. But he knew that her gradual improvement was natural and not on his account, and the heat did not come into his hands on the times he tried to ease her soreness again.

One morning, a few days after she had been able to feed the chickens for the first time without being troubled by any pain, Tommy put his hand up to his neck and felt a swelling there.

The burning pain in his stomach returned and he could not eat any food without it worsening.

*   *   *

The day he felt the pain in his belly, a woman came to the gate holding a small boy by the hand. The child's left arm was bent and twisted and his hand swollen, the joints of both his knees reddened. He had a rash on his hands and neck. Tommy sat with him for an hour. The heat did not come. The boy cried in pain and nothing helped him and the woman went away in tears too, though Tommy could not tell if they were of despair or rage.

'It has gone,' he said that night, and touched his hand to his neck.

'Surely not. Perhaps you have done too much and tried too hard.'

'No. I could have seen a hundred people in one day and it would not have made any difference.'

She looked at his face which was full of a strange sadness and of resignation.

Before long he was as ill as he had been before it all, tired and weak and in pain. He did not try to eat and only sipped water. Soon, he refused that too. He lay not in bed but on the old couch downstairs, and on the few warm periods of some late-autumn days, Eve left the door open so that he could feel the sun on his face and smell the earth that was turned as Bert Ankerby slowly dug over his garden ready for winter.

Eve sat silently beside him for hour after hour,

knowing everything, understanding nothing. He watched every movement she made.

People still came to the door and she gently turned them away and so word spread all over again, until they were left alone.

He asked her to promise that she would stay at 6 The Cottages, and then, a moment later, was sorry, it had been unfair to expect it, he told her, she should do whatever she wished.

'It was just that I would like to think of you here. At least for a year. But only if you would be happy.'

'I'd be happy nowhere else,' Eve said. For that was the truth, though she did not then know how she would manage it, for she had no work and rent must be paid.

He died in the dawn of a morning when the frost had crisped and whitened the grass and there was a thin skim of ice on the water trough. His pain had been very great but he had refused to let her send for the doctor for fear of gossip which might hurt or harm Eve.

The room was silent. Eve sat for a long time, without tears, looking out of the window.

Much later, when everything had been attended to, she walked out across the track and climbed the slope to the churchyard. There would be no blossom for many months and she came empty-handed, but knelt on the icy grass and traced her finger lightly over the lettering on the child's grave.

Jeannie Eliza Carr
Aged 3 years
Beloved daughter

Tommy could not be buried there. No one could now, and so she was obliged to have a plot in the town cemetery on the other side of the canal.

Word spread but perhaps not widely enough or else it did not speak with a loud enough voice and only Miriam and Bert and Mary Ankerby came to the funeral, with a handful of men who had once worked with Tommy and the usual gang of children, hovering on the other side of the cemetery wall and looking on with huge eyes.

Word had not spread to any of those he had helped out of pain and sickness, or if it reached them they turned deaf ears. But word reached the doctor, who felt vindicated, at first, for what he had said and believed, that there had not and could never have been, any healing and Tommy Carr had died of his illness, though later rather than sooner. But had died all the same. It was Eve he felt most sorry for, though Tommy had not been a bad man and had cared for his wife, that was without question.

179

But Tommy Carr was dead and it all would be forgotten and the sick of the town would come, as they had always come, to him.

'You won't go back there to be alone,' Miriam said as they walked away from the graveside.

'Where else would I go? That is home and always will be.'

'So you'll work to pay the rent.'

Eve did not answer. They had turned into Miriam's street and found the boys all outside, spilling over the kerb into the road with the baby's pram being raced up and down the pathway by three of the others.

Miriam screeched out to them to stop and they did so, running away and leaving the pram balanced on the kerb, the baby asleep and oblivious to it all. She sighed and hauled it back and Eve took the handle to push him to the front door.

'They could all be killed and what would he either know or care?'

Miriam had said nothing about Tommy, no word of kindness or affection, made no gesture of sympathy. She had come to the funeral. That was all.

'I'll have to make their tea,' she said now, taking over the pram.

'Thank you for coming there.'

'I would never have stayed away, how could you think that?'

'I didn't think it,' Eve said.

Her sister did not invite her in to share their tea or even just a cup.

Bert called from their door as she went by, asked her to go in to them. 'But maybe you'd rather just be on your own tonight and come to us another?'

'I would. But thank you and I will come. Later in the week I'd like to.'

He nodded and went in.

For a second, after the door of Number 5 closed, Eve felt entirely alone and bereft of anyone in the world. But she made herself tea and fed the chickens and then switched on the old wireless. There was dance music, which she liked and she knew that Tommy would not think her unfeeling.

Tommy.

It was not until the following week that she took enough courage to go through his few things and it was then she found the receipt for the year's rent on 6 The Cottages, folded carefully and tucked into his inside pocket. And the money. All that money.

She took it downstairs and laid it on the kitchen table under the lamp and knew everything then, though knowing was not understanding. He had been given something freely and passed it freely on, and when he had kept Mr Arnold's money, it had been withdrawn from him. That was how he had paid for this rent and for her blue scarf and the bar of rose soap. He had bought nothing for himself.

The gift had been withdrawn and with it his own health and strength. The pain and swellings and sickness had overwhelmed him and there were no more gifts.

But he was not to blame. How could he have been?

She sat on looking at the receipt for the rental, and the bar of rose soap wrapped in its pretty paper, lying on the table together, as the darkness drew in and a tawny owl hooted and the moon rose over the peak.

One night, a long time afterwards, she heard footsteps, steady on the path. She had been washing some of the china and looking for a clean cloth with which to dry it and polish it up to shine. It was early afternoon. She waited but for a moment there was silence outside. Since Tommy's death she had become strangely nervous sometimes, about being alone in the cottage and not only at night. She had no fear of spirits and in any case Tommy's spirit was always around her, she had nothing to be afraid of in that.

And then a soft knock on the door.

* * *

Arthur George had changed from a small boy into an older one. His face was beginning to form, the bone structure just visible beneath the still-soft round flesh. He had Miriam's eyes and his own withdrawn, slightly wistful air.

His jacket needed patching.

'Something has happened. What's wrong? Has your mother sent for you?'

'I came on my own.'

She opened the door wider and he walked quietly, almost hesitantly in, looking round as if he had never been in the place before, for all that he had known it since he was a baby.

'Would you like a glass of milk Arthur George?'

'Could I have a cup of tea?'

Eve smiled. 'There isn't a cake though.'

He looked disappointed. There was always a cake. She realised that she had not bothered because there was no one else here and what need had she of a cake to eat alone?

'I'll make a cake later. There's biscuits.'

He sat at the table and looked out of the door and down the path. 'The hens are laying then,' he said.

'They are – more than I can eat. You can take some back home with you.'

'I thought I wouldn't go home, just for a bit.'

'No, I meant later on. You're welcome. If there isn't anything wrong?'

'There's nothing . . .'

She set the sugary milky tea in front of him, as he liked it, and he began to dip a biscuit carefully in and stir it round as if it were a spoon, just pulling it out before it broke off, soft with liquid.

'Ha . . .' He smiled.

'You did that a long time ago.'

Eve had poured herself tea but sensed that he would not want to sit across the table with her and so she began to dry one of the rose-painted bowls.

'I could be handy,' Arthur George said.

'Handy.'

'I am. I can do a lot of things.'

'I know that. You've had to learn.'

'I'd be a help to you.'

She set the bowl down on the dresser. He was bolt upright on the chair, anxious eyes meeting hers. Eve went to sit down. She took a biscuit from the tin and after a second, dipped it into her tea. Arthur George watched and when she failed to catch it before it folded over into the hot drink and disappeared, banged his hand on the table and laughed with the glee of the small boy he had been so recently.

*　*　*

So that was the beginning of it, though she made him return home to tell his mother, as well as to fetch what things he needed.

'A short stay,' she said, as he went off, 'tell her you're coming for a short stay.'

He was back in not much more than an hour with a cloth holdall over his shoulder and watching him come brightly up the path to the open door, Eve was reminded of Tommy, saw Tommy in Arthur George, though of course they were not related.

But he had a look of Tommy and she clung to that.

It would not be a short stay. They both knew it. Did Miriam? If so, Eve knew her only thought would be that there was one less mouth to feed.

When he had gone to bed that night, after helping her shut up the hens and bolt the doors, Eve went to the dresser drawer, where she had put the money, took it out and counted it on the table. Money she had not known what to do with. But now she knew.

It was to be money for Arthur George, one day, for school or an apprenticeship. She had no idea how it might be used, what he would need and it scarcely mattered, for already he was what Tommy had been. A kind man, though still a boy. Another kind man.

Now read the first two chapters of Susan Hill's

The Beacon

'Magnificent . . . It is all done so well, so wisely, that this
short book is richly satisfying . . . a little masterpiece'
Daily Telegraph

'A brilliantly eerie little tale . . . with a very adroitly
handled contemporary theme' *Scotland on Sunday*

I

MAY PRIME had been with her mother all after-noon, sitting in the cane chair a few feet away from the bed, but suddenly at seven o'clock she had jumped up and run out of the house and into the yard and stood staring at the gathering sky because she could not bear the dying a second longer.

And when she returned only a little later Bertha was dead. May knew it had happened as she walked back into the house, before reaching the bedroom, before seeing her. She knew it from the change in everything and from the silence. But she still drew in her breath and her hand went to her mouth when she looked down.

The farmhouse was called the Beacon and they had been born and reared there, Colin, Frank, May and

Berenice, but only May had been left for the last twenty-seven years to live with both their parents and then, after their father's death, with their mother alone.

One week, their father had been helping to haul a cow out of a ditch and, the next, most of the animals had gone. Bertha Prime had called in a neighbour and had them sent to market. Only the chickens had remained.

After that, Bertha had let out the fields. Otherwise life had stayed the same. There were no animals to feed and milk early and late and, once Frank moved out, no man to do it anyway.

It was no longer usual, in the 1960s, for an unmarried girl to go on living with her parents, their insurance against the deprivations of old age, and if they had ever been asked about it directly, John and, after John, Bertha would have said that they would be more than happy for May to leave home, preferably to be married but if not that then for a career. They had neither asked nor expected her to remain with them. It had just happened.

May would have said the same. It had just happened. 'Fallen out that way.' There was more to it than that, of course, but John and Bertha did not know the 'more' and May preferred to bury it.

Perhaps Bertha guessed something but if she did she never spoke of it.

She stood in the doorway, hand to mouth, and her mother lay in the bed with the slatted oak frame and she was dead. From that moment everything was different. She was a dead body, not Bertha, not her mother.

May had been with her, watching from the front porch, when they had brought her dead father home and carried him up and laid him down on this same bed, so she knew the appearance of death, as she recognised the absoluteness of the silence. But it was shocking all the same. She went unsteadily across the room and sat in the cane chair, but for several minutes could not look at the bed.

2

J OHN AND Bertha Prime had taken the Beacon over from John's father and mother, and had moved in as one family in the last years of the thirties, and to Bertha living with them was what she had expected and the hard work was expected too. She had not come from a farming family – her parents had kept the village store – but no one could have lived at the Beacon without understanding what the life of everyone around them entailed. Only the large landowners had cottages into which sons and their new families could sometimes move. John Prime's father, also John Prime, was no such man.

John and Bertha had come back from their wedding straight to the attic bedroom, which had been turned out and cleaned in their honour, with new curtains and a new mattress for the old bed but nothing else, and the following morning Bertha had come downstairs to work in the dairy with her new mother-in-law. After the dairy there were the chickens and then the geese, and after the geese the beehives, and after that the kitchen, and that was life at the Beacon. Once a week she spent an afternoon with her own parents and served in the store, and at first it felt as if she had never left but, before long, this was changed and that was changed, things were in a new place, the shelving was rearranged, and Bertha had soon felt like a stranger who knew nothing of the way things should be.

They were married in July and in November she stopped going to the store every week and when she did go, she no longer served there because she got in the way and slowed things down, they said, and besides, now she was pregnant with her first child.

The baby, a boy, was born on the hottest day of the following summer while every available man and woman was out in the fields and Bertha lay and sweated in the attic bedroom through thirteen hours of labour. John Prime lived for half an hour only, and the next summer another baby was stillborn, though this one came in the night of torrential rain that washed a ton of mud and stones down the hill and half a flock of sheep were buried.

Her mother-in-law was not unfeeling, not unkind,

but having lost three children of her own, accepted those things as inevitable and said very little, though she did not press Bertha to return to the dairy or the kitchen, but let her work things out in her own time. But sitting alone in the attic or going for silent walks along the lanes and through the fields near the Beacon gave her thoughts of death, and when her mind turned twice to drowning and she caught herself looking at the strong branch of a tree, Bertha went back at once to work in the dairy and among the chickens, terrified.

Her husband, John, was sympathetic but uncomfortable and in any case spent little time with her, because there was always too much work to be done and that was the way of it. Only sometimes in winter, when the weather was bad and the nights drawn in, he would come with his father to sit beside the fire next to her and drink a glass of ale and talk a little, though always about the farm or the state of the land or the prices at market. Once or twice they would listen to the wireless and afterwards talk would turn to the wider world and what would happen if there was another war, as seemed likely. But the talk was brief and petered out with the dying fire and then it was time for the women to set out the bread and cheese and last drinks before bed.

Two days before the outbreak of war, Bertha went

into a short, sharp labour with Colin, who was nine pounds of furious health, and barely a year later Frank was born and a family was established and no one looked back, though Bertha went to the churchyard every Easter and Christmas to put flowers on the infant graves. In the years when she had been ill and first housebound and then bedridden, May had taken over the duty, because she was asked and because it was something that had just always been done like so much else in a life filled with habit and custom and a small amount of ritual.

May herself arrived in the spring of 1942, born in the same bedroom but only just, for by now Bertha's labours were even quicker and the baby had almost been born in the kitchen and then on the last treads of the stairs.

May was neither large nor robust but a long, pale, straggling baby who would not suckle and seemed to have no appetite for life. In the end, it was her grandmother who coaxed her forward a little further each day when Bertha's milk had run out, by giving the baby milk fresh from the cow and sitting patiently with her on a kitchen stool until she had finished a bottle. The two boys thrived and raced about.

Because their lives were already hard, the war brought nothing very much worse, and indeed, in some ways it was easier because it brought extra help on all the farms, in the shape of prisoners of war and even land girls, though the latter were never sent to the Beacon. The Prime family were better off for food than many others – the men shot rabbits and there were always fruit and mushrooms for those who knew where to look.

May was three when her grandfather died and she remembered nothing of him but the smell of his tobacco which seemed to come from the pores of his skin and the hair of his head and be woven like another layer of thread into every item of his clothing. When he died, John Prime moved into his shoes and the only difference was that now he gave instead of took the orders. The work was just the same. But there was never any question of John and Bertha moving out of the attic down to the big bedroom and the large bed. If the widow had ever felt it was her place to give them up now to the next generation, as others would and had in her position, she said nothing and did nothing and so everything remained as it had and Bertha could not ask. It was another ten years before Bertha attained the large room and the biggest bed, and by then she had forgotten that they had once been so prized. The attic was hers. The attic was where her marriage had begun, the attic was her marriage's own private space, her small world, and in the end she was reluctant to leave it. But by then Colin and Frank needed a bigger room and May moved into theirs, and so everything changed and life went on with only a pause for the shifting of mattresses.

They kept dairy cows and a few beef cattle, sheep and pigs and chickens, with geese and turkeys for Christmas, and they grew wheat and barley and potatoes, and as the land was partly on the side of the hill that stretched away from the Beacon and partly on the plain running down to the river, the work was both varied and never-ending. After the war they stopped using horses and bought a tractor and the milking gradually became more mechanised, but that did not shrink the working hours and the weather was against them for seven months of the year in this distant and uphill place.

May had fragmented memories of growing up at the Beacon, like a series of pictures in an album except that sometimes the pictures had sound or came with their own smell and taste. Someone from the village brought a grandchild of the same age, Sylvia, and Sylvia and May had wandered out into the strawberry patch and eaten the fruit warm from the sun until their mouths were scarlet and their stomachs ached. The taste and the smell of the berries and the straw they rested in and the earth beneath it were there for the taking for the rest of May's life if she read or heard the single word 'strawberry'.

The pain in the back of her legs after climbing the hill and the feel of the rain and wind stinging her face.

Her grandmother's smell when she was old. May had not liked to go near her in the chair or in her bed because of the smell which was of something both decaying and oddly sweet.

She had gone to school on the bus from the end of the track, but memories of school were even more fragmented. The feel of a wooden ruler in her hand and, once, being told that a girl in her class had measles very badly, and then next, that she was dead.

The shiny green tiles in the washroom. The cold water that made your teeth ache when you drank it from the tap, cupping your hand and filling it first then scooping the hand to your mouth.

But there were no really bad memories and that was important. Later, when she had to sit down and go step by step through her life – their lives – from far back to the present, she could not conjure up anything that was more than a passing unpleasantness that went with everyone's childhood – pain in a tooth or a boil or disappointment over something postponed. Life had simply gone on uneventfully until, when she was six, her sister and the last child had been born and christened Berenice. Sheila had been their grandmother's chosen name; John Prime would have gone along with anything. No one quite knew where Bertha had found the name Berenice.

From the beginning, May had loved her with a protective and slavish intensity, spending every moment she could hanging over the cot and the pram, answering her cries with an urgency that everyone said would be regretted. The baby had seemed complacent and self-absorbed and as she grew up had taken her sister's attentiveness so much for granted that it had warped her character. But May had continued to love and serve, and secretly, Bertha had found it a relief not to have more work, more calls on her attention. She had realised very quickly that the baby could be left to May.

May Prime was clever. That had been clear when she had picked out letters on the back of her father's newspaper as he held it up and then found the same letters in the family Bible and in the stock book and in the books from the glass case in the sitting room. She had found pencil and paper and copied the groups of letters until they formed words and asked for the words to be read and whispered them over and over, staring at the marks until they gave up their secret to her and she could read. That had been before she went to school and was a thing unheard of in the family, though both her grandmother and Bertha Prime read books during the winter and her father went through the paper from front to back every day after dinner.

She had loved to read and later to take the arithmetic books from her brothers and try to work out the exercises, though numbers did not make the same sense to her that words did. There was a globe of the world in the front room, beside the single glass-fronted case of books – Shakespeare, Sir Walter Scott, an encyclopedia, a dictionary, *Everyman in Health and Sickness*, the prayer book, *The Ready Reckoner*. She sometimes took down the globe and twirled it on its stand and read the names of the countries aloud.

By the time she went to school with Colin and Frank she could read and had an odd, random confetti in her brain of bits of knowledge which floated about and changed shape like the tiny shards of bright glass inside her brother's kaleidoscope. In the end the fragments would come together in a linear form, though some would prove incorrect or useless and others were lost altogether.

She loved the school from the first moment of walking into the cloakroom and finding her own name on a piece of card slotted into a little metal holder above a peg. Her name. She loved the smell of the entrance and the different, wood-dust smell of the hall and the smell of the classrooms which were placed all around it, a different smell again, of chalk dust and of other children.

She fell into schoolwork. She loved the exercise books she was given, one of which had times tables, rules and measures on the back, the other lists of the principal rivers and mountains of the world, of Kings and Queens, of Important Dates and Capital Cities and the Constellations. She learned them by heart without trying because she looked at them so often, read them so many times, that her mind, almost her skin, simply absorbed them.

As she moved up from class to class everything became more interesting and the exercise books now had algebraic and chemical formulae and French and Latin verbs. The beginning of each term, when she wrote her name on each book, filled her with a huge excitement for the knowledge that was waiting for her, the exercises to come.

Yet she was a friendly girl too; she learned skipping games and five stones and catching rhymes and huddled against the wall hearing tales. She played rounders because she had an excellent ball eye, though her running was awkward. She could jump higher than any other girl in the school and played the recorder well enough to be in the band.

When she was seven she acquired a particular friend who had come to the school that term.

Patricia Hogg's father was the new gamekeeper to the big estate on the other side of the hill, across the valley from the Beacon, and for a time, May, Patricia Hogg and a girl called Geraldine were always closeted together. But, three being a crowd, Geraldine was edged out, and May and Patricia Hogg were left to sit together, eat lunch together, walk part of the way home together. Patricia Hogg was a reader like May and in spring and summer they took their library books and sat in the sun on the wall or on the grassy bank, skirts hitched up above their knees so their legs would brown.

Patricia Hogg had none of May's fire for learning and the books she read were always school or fairy stories, but they formed a comfortable pairing.

Once, May was invited to stay with Patricia Hogg at the gamekeeper's cottage, which sent Bertha into a spasm of uncertainty and alarm, for no member of the Prime family had been to stay at the house of anyone who was not a close relative as far back as anyone could remember, so that there was the worry of what state May's clothes were in and how she should carry them and if presents ought to be taken.

But in the end this was sewn and that was mended and everything was clean and a canvas bag found in one of the upstairs trunks and a jar of honey and a slab of home-cured bacon wrapped in greaseproof and settled among the cotton knickers and white socks.

She had left with Patricia Hogg after school, walking importantly out of the gate carrying the canvas bag. They walked to the opposite end of the village from the one which led to the Beacon, and waited in the sun for a bus. When it came it was full with people coming back from the market and they had to stand, holding onto the cracked leather seat backs and swaying about as the bus went round the bends. She could remember the feel of the leather in her hand, years afterwards.

The cottage was on the very edge of the estate and backed onto the woods. It was small and dark with low ceilings and you went in straight from the street. There was no porch.

There were five of them living in the cottage with the indoors dog and two cats, and with May it was crowded and felt more so when the gamekeeper came in from work. He was a huge man. They were all huge, with large hands and feet, and Mrs Hogg had a great, wide backside which seemed to fill half the kitchen when she bent over.

May slept in the same bed as Patricia. She had never in her life slept in a bed with anyone else and crept to the far side and held onto the edge in case their legs touched. To May, sharing a bed was a strange and unpleasant thing to do, and hot, too, under the heavy quilt.

The Beacon was never completely silent because of being high up and always troubled by a wind, but here the woods seemed to press into the house like baize, so that no air could get through and the light was oddly green. She could not get to sleep for the stillness and the odd shrieks of creatures out in the darkness, and then she began to want the lavatory. She tried to ignore the pressure of it but in the end she had to whisper to Patricia, and not knowing what to say, asked, 'Has your dad locked up downstairs?'

The toilet was outside at the bottom of the thin garden close to the trees.

'Why, what are you frightened of?'

'I'm not frightened. I need to go to the toilet.'

'There's something under the bed for that.'

May had been mortified. There were pots under the beds at home too, though also a proper flush toilet in a lean-to beyond the scullery. The idea of using a pot with someone else in the room, even in the dark, was quite shocking. She lay absolutely still on the far edge of the bed and in spite of the discomfort eventually slept. She woke sometime later. It was still pitch black, and Patricia was making tiny snorting sounds. May slid inch by inch from the bed onto the floor and then felt around for the pot on the rough boards, praying for the other girl not to wake.

In some ways everything at the Hoggs' cottage was familiar. The dark. The fact that the outside world seemed to be inside too, the sounds the pigs made and the smells. Otherwise, it was entirely strange, denser and closer, as if everyone and everything was packed tightly together, bodies and clothes, china and pans, cats and chairs and the gamekeeper's guns and sticks.

There were the indoor dog, and two cats, but no animals other than two pigs and the gun dogs which lived in outside cages and the ferrets, and the wood came right to the fence and one day might have marched into the house like a wood in a fairy story.

May learned an early lesson about people, which is that they can change according to their settings and how they fit into them. Patricia Hogg at home was not the same as the one she knew at school. At home she took the lead and was not always friendly, sulked and was cocky. She was the eldest child of three and the only girl.

They went for desultory walks and sat in the fringes of the wood among leaves and pine needles with their backs against the tree trunks. May had brought a book but Patricia did not want to read. She did not seem to want her here and there was nothing to talk about.

They had been shooed out of the house after breakfast.

It was a dismal three days and May felt that she was doing wrong simply by being her usual self, but she had no other self to present and found herself, for the first but not the last time, without resources and unable to mould herself to blend with her surroundings or to fit in with the expectations of others. She had no idea what those expectations were. The difference in the other girl was both a shock and a puzzle and she did not know how to relate to this new Patricia Hogg.

She finished her book and asked if she could borrow another but there was only the Bible in the cottage, so she found herself reading Exodus and Isaiah and Revelation by the light of the oil lamp at the kitchen table while they drank beakers of cocoa and Mrs Hogg banged the iron down onto sheets and shirts. Always after, that biblical language was associated for May with the smell of the hot flannel and the dusty taste of cocoa so that wafts of one or the other came to her if she was in church or heard the Bible being read aloud anywhere.

The weekend with Patricia Hogg taught her so much that she was still absorbing the lessons months later. She learned about how differently others live and speak to one another, that friends can be slippery and friendships treacherous and that you needed to have resources within yourself to make up for it.

Inevitably, her friendship with Patricia changed and they spent less time together, and when the question of her coming in turn to the Beacon was raised, May was at first evasive and later, when it recurred, said that Patricia was afraid of sleeping in strange houses. She knew that her mother was quietly relieved. There was enough to do and more without the anxiety of having a visitor.

During May's last years at the village school her friendships were more numerous and also more casual, and in any case she was focusing on the scholarship to the grammar school which would take her away from many of the people she had been with from the beginning. She longed for the senior school, longed for the new lessons and the new books, the uniform and the opening out of world upon world. It was taken for granted that she would pass the examination and so she believed it and made plans in her mind accordingly. The others would go to the secondary school in the market town; the grammar was fifteen miles and a much longer bus ride away. During the final term and after the exam, May detached herself from the village school and everyone in it little by little, though no one else was aware of it.

She did so instinctively and to harden herself, not wanting to be hurt by the pain of the final separation. It was the place she would miss and the loss of it would affect her no matter where she went next, for the small building was what she had loved the most, and although she was eager for her future and the new life, she did not yet know what the new school was like or how strong an attachment she might develop for it.

At home, nothing changed outwardly but Berenice grew and in growing she too began to reveal herself. She was a spoilt and manipulative child, prone to tears and tantrums and to sudden fevers which gave her fits and caused terror in everyone other than May, who had a calm inner knowledge that Berenice would always survive. No mere physical illness, no fever however high and dramatic would ever get the better of her – that much was perfectly clear to May, though to May alone. And yet May loved her as much now that her true nature was visible as she had when Berenice had been a quiet and undemanding baby, and Berenice accepted her sister's attentions and love as her due and was nourished and enriched by it.

May loved her brother Colin because he was so easy, so straightforward, so readable and predictable. Life for Colin was an uncomplicated business because it was entirely outward. He had, apparently, no inner life whatsoever, no private thoughts or concealed feelings, no complex responses to other people or to events. Life was linear. Colin had no favourites and no secrets, he treated everyone according to their status in the hierarchy, looked to himself, was generous and hard-working and ended every day in every way the same as he had begun it.

And then there was Frank.